Class

Reunion

The Sequel to Thornhill High School

A novel by Jeffery Roshell

Class

Reunion

RoWash Publishing Presents:

CLASS REUNION

Author: Jeffery Roshell

ISBN-13: 978-1729746974

ISBN-10: 1729746977

LCCN: TBD

Editing/Typesetting: Young Dreams Publications – Ty Waller
www.youngdreamsbig.com

FOREWORD

As a book club President, I get the opportunity to meet and interact with authors on a daily basis. Although it is a pleasure to meet all authors, I especially enjoy meeting new authors. They are very passionate about their work and future opportunities. My book club has been together for six years and I love to introduce them to a new author's work. I try my best to include as many new authors in our book of the month line up as I possibly can. I met the author of this novel, Jeffery Roshell, nearly two years ago through social media. I followed his progress as he began writing his first novel, *Thornhill High School*. He was extremely determined and set many goals for himself throughout the process. From what I can tell, he has successfully completed those goals and more! He has been very supportive of me and my endeavors and I do everything I can to support him as well. He is also very supportive of others in the literary industry and that is a very admirable quality. I was so pleased when his first novel was completed and could not wait to read it. I was not disappointed. It was filled with all of the drama and chaos that you could imagine coming from a group of high school students navigating the winding road from adolescence to adulthood. His writing style was so vivid; at times I felt that I was inside of the story with the rest of the characters in the novel.

In *Class Reunion*, the Thornhill High School crew is back! Kenvarius (KJ), Corrine and Angie are all returning for their ten year reunion. Normally, I try to avoid my own class reunions but there is no way I could miss this one! After leaving us with so many jaw dropping moments in *Thornhill High School*, it is only right that Mr. Roshell takes us back into their world. After finishing the first book, I had so many questions. I absolutely had to know what happened next with these characters. Are they still together? What happened with Angie's situation? Did the parents approve or were they shocked and angry? Did he stick around? How did she feel when she found out or was it hidden? All of these questions and more have been running through my mind since I finished *Thornhill High School*. In *Class Reunion*, someone is back on the scene and they are out for revenge. I have a few ideas of who this may be but with this author, you can never be too sure of an outcome. As soon as you think you have the plot figured out, he puts a twist in it that makes you say, "Did that really just happen?" This story could only be told by this author because he has a way of combining comedy, drama and chaos together while topping it off neatly with a message that can be used in our daily lives. His characters are so believable and down to earth, I'm sure that most of us can relate to a lot of the things that they experienced.

Jeffery Roshell came onto the writing scene with grit and determination. His hard work has definitely paid off. He won the APS Books Fiction Novel of theYear Award in 2017 for his second novel, *It's Gonna Rain* and also delved into the world of Erotica with his third book, *Friday After Dark*. In such a short amount of time, he has proven himself to be a serious writer and has definitely earned a seat at the table. Soapbox moment: It is so important for us to support authors. Especially authors that produce great books that keep us entertained. Here are several ways to show support: Buy the book, review the book, tell a friend or two or three about the book and share it on your social media pages and blogs if you have them. All of these things can be done in the comfort of your own home and the author will appreciate your effort in helping them spread the word about their book(s). With that being said and without further ado, let's get ready to turn the page and jump back into the lives of Kenvarius (KJ), Corrine, Angie and the rest of the Thornhill squad. Grab your favorite beverage, sit back, relax and prepare to go on a ride that will be nothing short of wild and entertaining.

Blessings,

Kenya Ervin, President

Soul Sistahs Book Club

Chattanooga, TN

Dedicated to all those who requested this follow-up Sequel…

2009

CORRINE

"Thanks, Brenda! And I will see you on the twenty-first for the Black Author's Fair in Miami. Okay, talk with you soon, bye."

I hit the end button on my Blackberry phone and laid it on my marble kitchen counter. I looked out the window to the view of the palm trees and water. It was already a sunny, blazing eighty-five degrees on a Friday morning in August. The Coral Ridge neighborhood of Ft. Lauderdale had been my home for the past four years. It was the happily-ever-after life that God granted me after graduating from college, becoming a New York Times bestselling author, and NBA star's wife. Life couldn't be even more surreal. Suddenly my phone starts to ring which startled me out of my daze. I smiled at the number and photo that came across the screen.

"Hello," I answered with a broad smile across my face. I turned on the speakerphone.

"Bae, wassup?"

"Good morning. Mr. Lexington." I responded and smiled again. I got up grabbed a fresh plum from the refrigerator, and sat back down at the table.

"Well, I should be pullin' up in about fifteen minutes. Happy to be home from the Nike Shoot." He responded.

"How was L.A.?" I asked.

"Great! Got a chance to hang with a few celebrities after the Nike shoot. I had a good time. How's my favorite New York Times bestselling wife?"

"Great! Brenda just called about the Miami Black Author's Book Fair on the twenty-first. I am the featured author and keynote speaker. I am really excited about that." I say with great

excitement. It really had been a journey being on this author road. I

had published a total of four novels, and my latest just made the

New York Times Bestseller's list.

"That's good news, bae. You know, I can't believe it's already

near the end of 2009. Our high school reunion is this time next

year. It will be ten years that we have been out of high school."

K.J. says.

As he's talking about the reunion, I began to think about how I

missed Chicago and Parkersville, and the memories of attending

Thornhill High School, my teenage years – it all ran rapidly in my

head. "K.J. don't remind me," I said shaking my head at the fact

that time had flown by just that quick. I couldn't believe that I

finally became the adult I wanted to become so badly back then.

How I wished like hell I could go back and be a teenager again.

"Well, Clevon has been blowing my phone up asking when we

are coming home. I told him at least not until November for

Thanksgiving since the team has no game that week. It's going to be nice to see the newly built gym I had put on the school." K.J. says.

I smiled again, thinking about the recent sixty- thousand dollar donation that K.J. gave for Thornhill High School. A newly built state-of-the-art main gym with a fitness center for the school athletic department. All of the athletic teams received brand new uniforms, and the track turf around the football field has been painted red with a gold stripe in the middle going all around. And to top it off, an entirely new football stadium, press box, and the home side football bleachers had been painted red, black, and gold. The baseball diamond had been re-done, and the marching band, flag girls, and dancing Centurionettes received new uniforms in honor of winning the national title. The Chicagoland news stations and Essence Magazine recognized K.J. for his contributions, praising him through live media coverage and articles.

As you can see life has been a fairytale for the both of us for the last almost ten years. It felt like it was just yesterday he had given me his number in our eighth grade P.E. class, and now I was his wife. Martha, our maid/nanny from Haiti, came walking into the kitchen holding our five-month-old baby girl, Kylie. Martha was about five-foot-seven, had a stocky build, fifty-eight years old, and she always wore her hair in a tight bun. Martha came to us about two years ago, and we have loved her since. She was like a second mother to all of us. She was more than a maid, she was part of the family, and I just loved her Haitian accent.

"Mrs. Lexington, I have given Kylie her morning bottle, bathed and changed her, now she is ready for mommie." Martha said handing her to me.

"Thank you, Martha!" I said smiling and taking Kylie out of her hands. Kylie smiled at me as I baby talked her. Suddenly I remembered I had K.J. on the phone. He surprises me by yelling Kylie's name. Kylie smiled as I put her in the high chair that Martha had brought out to the table where I was sitting. Motherhood was something that was new but awesome to me. Reminiscing on all the stories my mother used to tell me about myself growing up, now that I was finally a parent I found myself in some similar situations. My mother loved Kylie and could not wait for us to get home so she could see her grandbaby. She was

5

itching for some youth in the house because my twin brothers
Ceron and Coron were well into law school - soon getting ready to
graduate and then take the bar exam. Both my parents were thrilled
for them. Becoming lawyers was a significant accomplishment for
our family.

I got up to get some applesauce to feed Kylie when I noticed
the line had clicked and I saw K.J.'s Ferrari pull up with him
jumping out and gathering his things.

"It's good to be back in the M. I. A.!!!" K.J. yelled coming
through the doors and sitting his bags down. I went over to him
and gave him a kiss and a hug, after which Kylie started reaching
for him, and he walked over to her and picked her up.

"Good to have you home Mr. Lexington." Martha said as she
washed and dried her hands. She started to heat up the breakfast
that she had made for the both of us on the stove.

"Martha, appreciate you. You're like a mother!" K.J. said as he
walked over to her and hugged her with Kylie still in hand. He then
came back and handed Kylie to me, kissed me on the cheek, and

went and grabbed his bags and started to head toward the stairs.

"Bae, I'm going to shower and then come back and talk with you."

"Okay," I responded as I put Kylie back in her high chair. I took another look out of the window. Martha came over and sat down a plate of turkey bacon, scrambled eggs, and a few pieces of cut up apples, oranges, and grapes, along with a glass of white grape juice. I smiled at her picking up my fork to start eating. But then it hit me, there was someone who I had not talked to in a while. I picked up my cell phone, dialing out quickly.

ANGIE

"I'm Sylvia Matthews and welcome to another edition of E Entertainment. Today we talk with up-and-coming NBA star, Gino Aiello who has overcome the odds of becoming a young father growing up in Parkersville, Illinois to now the next best thing to Kobe Bryant in the NBA."

"You have got to be fuckin' kidding me." I said to myself. I watched the bullshit, lying interview and quickly picked up my cordless house phone after it was over.

"Hello?" Gino said picking up after three rings.

"I really wish that you would stop telling these news reporters that you had this hard ass life! You grew up on the west side of

Parkersville. That area was then, as it damn sure still is now, very decent and expensive to live in! You went to West-South, still the number one high school in the south suburbs of Chicago when it comes to demographics and education. So, explain to me why you keep telling the media you had a hard upbringing? I was the one who sacrificed my four-year education at U of I. I had to go to Chicago State University, not to mention work a full-time call center job and take care of a baby while you went away to Stanford, graduated, and then went off to the NBA. So, please tell me, who was the one that had the hard-ass life?" I got all that out in one breathe over the phone, waiting on Gino to respond.

"Angela? Did you really call me to ask me this for the thousandth time? I do not draw up these interviews. They ask me questions, and I answer them." He said.

"That's bullshit! And you know it! Tell them the truth because it's all lies. You acknowledge the fact that you have a son, but you do not mention anything about me, and what really happened!" I yelled sitting up on the loveseat in my living room.

"Angela, you have been brought up several times in interviews I have done in the past, on several different occasions. I am not about to do this with you again this morning. Is Mannie around?" Gino asked sarcastically.

"Mannie!" I yelled out to our nine-year-old son. After a while, he came flying down the steps from his bedroom upstairs.

"Yes, mom?" He said.

"It's your daddy." I responded handing him the cordless phone. He took the phone out of my hand and started talking to Gino.

The only thing good that came out of our situation was our son. I thought back to my high school graduation day when I found out I was pregnant. During the ceremony I collapsed on the stage when my name was called to receive my diploma from dehydration, not even knowing that I was a month pregnant in the first place. My mother rushed me to the hospital and the shock we both were in to find out I was pregnant. My mother immediately took me to Gino's house to share the news. We carried my grandmother with us just in case some extra shit jumped off with them hearing that Gino was about to be a father. My mother wasn't even pleasant about it. She got to the party, and immediately blurted it out in front of his invited guest and his immediate family at his graduation party. Everyone was shocked, Gino's mouth dropped down to the floor, and he damn near passed out.

We met because we were both a part of a co-tutoring program that both our schools partnered up to do. I was Gino's peer tutor. I took on the task because it went on my high school record, which looked good to colleges, especially the one I was supposed to attend - the University Of Illinois Champaign-Urbana. Tutoring him at first was a nightmare, but he started to get the concept of Algebra II and Trig. He needed to get a passing grade to go off to Stanford University where he had gotten a scholarship to play basketball. We eventually started to notice a physical attraction for each other and we acted upon it. I wanted to be acknowledged as his girlfriend, he promised me that he would. On the day that I was supposed to be announced as such, I was invited to a dinner at his home by his mother. Turns out his ex-girlfriend had come back in the picture, which he failed to let me know. I was hurt and swore him off for good. Unfortunately for me, I ended up pregnant. I honestly thought his parents were going to have an issue with it because I am Black and Gino is Italian. But surprisingly, his mother and I became very close during my pregnancy. She loves Mannie to death, and so does his father.

I looked at Mannie observing his vanilla colored skin, his boxed, buzzed haircut like Paulie D from the MTV show Jersey Shore, and his light grey eyes. I could not believe how the time was flying - he would be ten years old before I knew it. And he looked just like Gino had spit him out him damn self. I'd admit that looking at him sometimes would drive me fucking crazy because he looked so much like his father.

We lived in a three-bedroom home in Frankfort, Illinois which was about twenty minutes from my old neck of the woods, Parkersville. I worked as a full-time Geometry teacher at my old high school Thornhill, also in Parkersville. Not only that, I had just taken on the role of head varsity cheerleading coach, after my old coach Vernita Davis who had been the head coach for the last ten years. She finally stepped down from her coaching and teaching positions at Thornhill. She'd made the decision to move out of state. She passed the baton onto me as I transitioned up from coaching the junior varsity squad to the varsity squad. Mannie attended a private Catholic school with some of the local celebrity and Politian's kids in the area. Gino wanted it that way, paying that expensive ass tuition for Mannie to attend there.

"Mom, dad wants to talk to you." Mannie said handing me the phone.

"Yes?" I said putting it up to my ear and changing the channel on my DIRECTV box.

"I would like to stop these altercations when we talk on the phone around Mannie. That's not healthy for him to hear us arguing all the time, Angela. Better yet, stop callin' me every time you see me on the damn TV."

"Stop your fabricated stories then I will." I rebutted back. Gino made a sighing noise and told me he had to get back to his trainer and would talk with me later. I said "uh-huh" and hit the end button on the phone. Mannie sat down next to me, and I looked at him and smiled. My baby was becoming a big boy on me.

"Dad said he's gonna send me the new the Kobe Bryant's. I got to have them for basketball camp, ma!" He said with excitement.

"Your daddy needs to stop spoiling you, sir." I said leaning over and pulling him into a motherly hug and kissing him on his cheek. He hated when I did this.

"Come on, ma." He replied as he slightly pushed me away.

I laughed. Mannie had everything that an only child could ever want. If Gino didn't buy him any and everything, then it was my mother or grandmother, or Gino's mother and father spoiling him with video games, toys, clothes, and expensive gym shoes. Mannie jumped up and went back upstairs. I told him to get in the shower and get some clothes on because we were going to the mall today. I wanted to enjoy these last free summer days before I went back to work at Thornhill. It was almost time for the new school year and coaching the varsity cheerleaders. I heard my Blackberry start ringing. I grabbed it and smiled when I saw who was calling.

"Well look who decides to finally give somebody a damn call back." I said giving playful attitude.

"Hey, now you know I've been busy with the book, and now that it's finished I can take a breather. But what's going on?" Corrine my best friend since grade school said.

"Nothing. Just got off the phone with Gino's ass. He did another one of them, *woe is me, I was a young father going into college, but now I'm one of the top young NBA players* interviews. I'm tired of his ass making it seem like he had a hard life." I said.

"Girl, I saw that one he did a few weeks ago with Sports Center. I could do nothing but shake my head."

"Please, he wants to stay relevant since the L.A. Seventy-Sevens can't win an NBA Championship, let alone play." I said and Corrine laughed.

"But anyway, so the book is done, huh? Can't wait to read it."

"Yes, finally! The publishing house and Brenda, my agent, are both off my ass now. I can rest and relax for a few months, and you know me and K.J. will be there soon." Corrine said.

"Hell, yes! I haven't seen you since January around my birthday, and I wanna see my Kylie-mama!" I said getting up and stepping on one of Mannie's toys as I walked fast to the kitchen. "Damnit, Mannie!" I yelled as the toy car he had on the floor hurt the bottom of my foot. "I done told him about these toys." Corrine laughed and I asked her what the fuck was funny, and jokingly told her to wait 'til Kylie starts doing the same shit to her.

"Girl, I got a little minute. A little minute before Kylie even starts walking." Corrine was quiet for a moment. "So, it's been ten years. You ready for this class reunion?" She asked.

I sat back on the couch and shook my head. I took an intense short five seconds to breathe and replied, "Hell to the no!"

"Angie, why not?" Corrine asked shocked.

"Girl, I don't wanna see nobody. Hell, I really don't wanna go. I see most of the ones who didn't move out of state either at the mall, stores, or they got little sisters, brothers, cousins, nephews, nieces, god kids, etc. that are now at Thornhill. I can't escape these people. They be at the games, PTO meetings, and parent-teacher conferences all the time. I am not excited about it at all!"

Corrine got quiet again. The truth of the matter was I still was embarrassed from when I collapsed on the stage at graduation; I did not want to face anyone at this class reunion. I really didn't want anyone to bring it up.

"Anyways, I know that is not your final answer. You're going if I gotta drag your ass out of the house." She said.

"Changing the subject, tell K.J. on behalf of The Thornhill High School staff and students, we say thank him very much for the contributions that he did for the school recently! Especially the cheerleaders, we did not have to do any fundraisers to get money for new varsity regular and competition season uniforms."

"When did there start to be a need for competition uniforms?" Corrine asked.

"That's the new thing, girl. You have regular football/basketball season uniforms and also a separate uniform for competition season for the teams. Even now the junior varsity is

17

even competing in junior varsity competitions now. Cheerleading

has changed since we were in high school almost ten years ago." I

said turning off the TV and walking up the stairs to my master

bedroom to get ready for the day that I had planned with Mannie.

"Well you would think as being captain, I would know and

have stayed up on this. I know you're just as shocked that you are

head coach now?" Corrine asked.

"Now you know the last place I thought life would take me

would be back to Thornhill teaching and also coaching the varsity

cheerleaders. But I love it! But did you and K.J. hear and see what

Stanley Brown did for West-South?" I asked going into the

bathroom in my master bedroom.

"No, what happened?" She asked.

"I knew it was something that I had meant to tell you since we

last seen each other. Well, Stanley decided to make a contribution

of his own for West-South. No, he didn't donate money for a new

gym, sportswear for the teams, lunchroom, or something small.

No, not Stanley Brown. He goes and has a whole new high school built for them!" I said.

"Whaaaatttttttt?" Corrine screamed.

"Girl, yes! Which has also changed the boundary lines for Thornhill and West-South students. You know where Cotreece's old house is before the bridge which is considered the ending border for Thornhill, the beginning for West-South?"

"Yeah?" Corrine said really engaged in the conversation.

"Well, that is now considered the starting point for West-South where she used to live. But it gets better…" I said sitting down at my makeup counter looking in the mirror. This rivalry was really bringing back memories for Corrine. "The Floyd Homes have been divided. The first three buildings at the beginning of the entrance are all Thornhill, the last three all go to West-South now. And those white people that live on the west side of Parkersville are having a fit! So you see Stanley Brown really did a disservice by building this new million-dollar high school building. Although it can accommodate so many students, it has started a brand new

19

boundary divide for the district. West-South is still predominately white, but now you have some of the ghetto ass project, Floyd Homes kids going there. Like President Obama said *change has come!*" I said laughing.

"So what are they going to do with the old high school? And when do they go into this new building? Have you been over to see it?" Corrine asked.

"They're going to tear it down starting next week. The kids should be going into the new building at the end of the month when school starts, and I had seen it when they started construction on it last July. I have to admit it is very hot! Even their redone football stadium." I said.

"Well you know he got the money. I'm sure it was nothing for him. Wait 'til I tell K.J. about this. And that girl he married she's a model or something, right?" Corrine said.

"Yea, she's bi-racial, very pretty." I answered her back.

"Girl, this my momma. What you about to do?" Corrine asked cutting our conversation short.

"Getting in the shower and taking Mannie to the mall. Just call me later." I said getting up and gathering my Bath and Body Works Japanese Cherry Blossom shower gel and shower sponge to shower with.

"Okay, I will." She said quickly and I ended the call.

"Mannie?" I called out to him as he came dashing into my room.

"Yes, mama?" He answered.

"I just wanted to make sure that you were doing what I asked you." I said as he smiled at me and I smirked at him shaking my head. "But please make sure you do not leave any more toys out. I stepped on a Lego. Now be ready by the time I am out the shower." I said as he responded with "okay" and dashed back out to his room. He was probably on his PlayStation because he was already dressed and had showered. I turned on my Bose Entertainment Box, pressed play and an old Toni Braxton cut came on, and I proceeded to get in the shower.

CLASS REUNION

K.J.

"Baby you know I cannot wait until you and Corrine get here. Even though Walter and I were just down there in May, it seems like that was months ago." I listened to my mother talk on speakerphone as I was getting ready to go get a fresh lining at the barbershop. My mother had remarried a guy she met at church. They met during my sophomore year in college. I liked Walter he was really cool, and as long as he treated my mother right, I had no problems with him. Walter was an electrician, he had a daughter who was in her thirties from his previous marriage. After Max, our English Bulldog had died, I knew my mother was going to definitely need companionship. Soon as I and got into the NBA, she sold our old house and moved into a condo in the upscale neighborhood of Lindencrest with Walter. By the time Corrine and I married, my mom and Walter had already been married a year.

"I know, ma. I talked to dad the other day." I said changing topics.

"How is your father?" She asked.

"He's doin' ai'ight. He and Diana were just here in Miami last month for a few days. Diana's son is thinking about going to FAMU for school, and her daughter is about to marry some big time lawyer from Jersey." I said getting my Nike bag together as well because basketball practice was an hour after my hair appointment at the barbershop.

"Well, that's good to hear Kenvarius. I know you are just as excited about your class reunion next year?"

"Ma, I can't believe I've been out of high school ten years. It just seems like yesterday I was crossing the stage. And college ran right on by me as well."

"I told you it would. I told you that rushing and wanting to become an adult would eventually catch you quick. But I am so proud of you, you're in the NBA. Married and have a child of your own. The Lord has been good!" My mother said which made me smile.

I went rushing down the stairs to see that Corrine and Kylie had left. She told me that she had a meeting with the other basketball wives of the team today and their kids. Martha was in the living room cleaning. I went back up the steps and out the patio doors in the master bedroom to overlook the Miami scenery which was beautiful on the hot day.

I continued to converse with my mom, "Yes, the Lord has been good. Everything has come full circle. I am also happy that the Fahrenheit are not playing Thanksgiving weekend. Everybody is anticipating me, Corrine, and Kylie's arrival. I'm going to try to see as many people as I can that weekend." I said.

"Well, it should definitely be a good time when you come. But before you know it, you will be right back for your class reunion." My mother added.

I looked at the time and I had to make a move to get to the barbershop. I told my mother that I loved her, and would talk with her later ending our call. I gathered my phone as I closed the patio doors locking them. As I walked toward the master bedroom door, I looked at my old high school varsity basketball photo. Then another photo of the entire team and me, Corrine and the varsity cheerleaders when we won the state championship, and it seemed like 2000 was just here. I didn't know what to expect with this class reunion or how my classmates that I had not seen in the last ten years were going to look - or even if they were still alive. I grabbed my wallet off the dresser put it in my back pocket and went downstairs to let Martha know that I was leaving and would be back later.

JEFFERY ROSHELL

CORRINE

Finishing my interview and photo shoot with Essence
Magazine, I felt that I had just accomplished another major plateau
for the year of 2009. I was going to be featured on the cover, and
the topics that were discussed today ranged from me becoming a
National African-American bestselling author, motherhood, and
finally the life of a basketball wife. The dress that I spent over two-
thousand dollars for was stunning, adding to my hair and makeup
was done by Miami's own Capricia Jennings. One of the most
coveted stylist out. She often did rapper Trina's hair and makeup
and other notable Miami A-listers.

I returned home to for some relaxation and to enjoy my free time. Martha handed me a frozen peach margarita that she had made. I changed my clothing to some loungewear and decided to sit out in the back on the back patio to get some sun.

K.J. was at practice and wanting to call Angie was another thing on my mind, but she was already in her classroom teaching. I took a sip of the drink and then sat the cup down next to the lounge chair. Kylie was sleeping so I definitely was about to enjoy the quiet moments of the afternoon. I heard my phone buzz, I picked it up seeing that Brenda was texting me about how happy she was the Miami Black Authors Fair went. She also wanted to remind me that in three weeks I would be doing the morning show on Miami South 105.6 with radio host Carlitha Jay.

Smiling, I texted "Yes, and I could hardly wait!" With so much talk about the class reunion, I started going through boxes and found my yearbook from my senior year. Opening the book, memories began to fill my head as I turned pages with pictures of familiar faces and things. I even pulled out a few pics that were loosely in the book from homecoming, winter ball, Spring bling dance, and prom. I had not seen this book since I graduated college

five years ago.

ANGIE

"Jeffrey! Jeffrey, Poo-Poo!" There was silence on the other end. "Hello?" I called out making sure that he had picked up and the call did not disconnect.

"You know, I'm a grown ass man now! A grown ass man with kids to be exact. You would think that you would stop."

"No, as long as you are my brother, you will be Jeffrey Poo-Poo!" I said stopping at the red light and laughing.

"What's up?" He said sounding irritated.
"Nothing. On my way to mama's shop. She's about to do my hair finally." I said.

"Hey, Uncle Jeff." Mannie said chiming in.

"Watup Nephewwwwww!" Jeff responded.

As I made a left onto Birch Street coming up to Devlin Ave, I heard Jeff ask Mannie about school and how many little girlfriends he had. I quickly chimed in and said, "None because I didn't want to even think about my baby having a girlfriend at nine years old."

"How you know he ain't got no girlfriend?" Jeff asked.

"Cause, he don't need to be thinkin' bout no fast ass little girl right now. He's only nine years old!" I barked back.

"Your mama something else and I know this for a fact because I grew up with her." Jeff said laughing at the comment. Mannie smirked a little until he looked at me and I gave him a stare right back.

"I do have to tell you something." Jeff said changing the subject.

"And that is?" I asked him.

"Nette pregnant again…"

"What?" I roared, slamming on the brakes at the abrupt red light I came upon.

"Yeah, man!" He said.

I could tell he was feeling a certain kind of way. Anjanette, or Nette as we called her, was Jeffrey's wife. They already had five kids, and she and Jeff were only twenty-five years old. Four boys and one girl, my nephews and niece were five, four, three, two, and eighteen months. I could only imagine what my mother was going to say when she and my grandmother both found out. They both had told Jeff that Anjanette needed to have her tubes tied. The five kids were enough, but here it was again now that she would be expecting a sixth child. They were too young for that many kids, and now they were about to welcome another edition - lucky number six.

"Jeff, what are you and Nette gonna do?" I asked him.

"Well, she finally thinks her tubes need to be tied."

"And they should. I only have one, and that sometimes feels like too much." I said to him approaching my mother's salon.

"Sis, who you tellin'? Well, hopefully, she goes with it. I don't want no more kids." Jeff says.

"You gonna be running around with grey hair at twenty-five. " I added laughing.

"Yeah, ai'ight." He came back at me with.

I turned into the parking lot of Ilene's Sass Number 2, my mother had been fortunate to open the second shop from the original one that she had been at since I was in high school.

"Don't say nothing to mama." Jeff said as I parked cutting off the ignition.

I put my Blackberry on speaker grabbing my purse. Mannie got out, and so did I. I hit the alarm on my 2007 Chevy Terrain.

"I'm quite sure she already knows." I added thinking about how news with Jeff and his wife traveled fast to my mother and grandmother because Nette would have already told somebody. She comes to mom's shop regularly to get her hair done. So I'm sure she would have already mentioned to her or somebody that worked at the hospital alongside my grandmother. Nette and my grandmother were registered nurses. I'd imagine that my grandmother and mother were waiting for me to get there so they could tell me all of their business.

"Nette promised me she wouldn't say shit this time." Jeff said just knowing that I probably was right.

I walked in right behind Mannie through the glass doors of my mother's shop. The Isley Brothers', *I Once Had Your Love (And I Can't Let Go)* blared out of the sound system. On the other side in the waiting area was the TV blasting a random show playing on B.E.T. There was a lot talking and laughter, hair getting done, nails being done, the shop was it's usual busy self. The second location was opened in 2005. Her original shop was opened in my old neighborhood. My mother co-owned that shop now with her good friend, because she spends most of her days here in the new site. The décor of the shop fit my mother's personality. There was a huge, beautiful oil painting of her on the wall. I remember her going on-and-on about how much the painting costed her. She had it alongside a sign that read *Illene's Sass #2*.

"Granny!!!" Mannie yelled running toward my mom, falling into her arms as she hugged him tightly.

"How's Na-na's man?" She said kissing him on the cheek with her red lipstick which left a mark on his light, bright cheek.

"Good." He responded as he then turned his attention to my grandmother who called out his name. He ran over to her and hugged her too. I set my purse down and grabbed a glass of champagne the front receptionist had poured. She also set out finger sandwiches, crackers, and cheese for the patrons who were there waiting to get their hair and nails done.

I put my earpiece in to hear Jeff. "Tell mama and granny I said hello, I'm about to get off the phone." Jeff said.

"Okay." I responded sipping from the glass and hitting the button on my earpiece. I told my mother and granny what Jeff had said, and immediately they both went in.

"So, Nette pregnant again?" My mother said setting up shop, getting ready to do my hair.

"She needs to see Dr. Kim." My granny added as she transitioned to the nail tech's chair from getting her mirco-braids styled in a high bun.

"I done told Jeff that's too many damn kids and they both ain't even thirty yet! I know I had him and Angie young, but that was it!" My mother said putting the cap around my neck and clipping the button.

"And I look good for a great-granny at fifty-seven!" My grandmother added laughing.

I looked at the both of them, shaking my head. This reminded me of being younger. They would always go on-and-on about how they were good mothers even though they had their children young. They always patted themselves on the back.

"Mama, can I go next door to see if Rodrick is ready to cut my hair?" Mannie asked looking just as innocent and handsome as he could for a nine-year-old.

"You have your phone on you?" I asked him as my mother started brushing out my hair so it could get washed and rinsed first.

"Yes." He replied.

"Alright. And if he's not, come right back. Them barbershop conversations are too deep for your young ears. And if Rodrick says you don't have to listen to me and that you can stay, I'ma come and slap the hell out of him." I said getting up and following my mother to sink counter.

"Okay." He said running out the door.

Rodrick was the owner of the barbershop, On Pointe Kutz, next door to my mother's shop. He treated Mannie like he was his little brother or nephew, and sometimes wouldn't charge me a thing for cutting his head.

"Well, I had gotten pregnant with Mannie right at the end of senior year. At least Jeff had his once he got out of high school." I said to my mother and grandmother as they both gave me crazy looks as to why I would make a comparison to me and Jeff's situations.

"Whatever! So are you excited about 2010 coming? Your class reunion is approaching." My mother asked.

"Not really. I mean I see the same people on Facebook and some of them have relatives that attend Thornhill. But it's Corrine that is really making me go." I said dryly.

"Angie why? Come on it's your class reunion. You truly have not changed at all and you kept that figure!" My granny said. Then she told the nail tech she wanted gold polish.

"Well, it's not that I really don't wanna go and shut it down with Corrine, I guess I'm just not excited about it. But who knows, once it gets closer to that time, then maybe I'll be more excited." I said.

"And hopefully by that time, you'll have a man to go with you." My granny said her, and the nail tech laughed like the bitch knew me.

"I don't need no man to go to the class reunion with me." I said as my mother started doing my hair when I moved back from the wash tub and into the chair. Her and my granny knew whenever they started talking about this, I was going to get mad.

"Angie, nobody is saying that you need a man to go to the reunion with you, but you have not had a real relationship in years. Don't you want more kids?" My granny asked.

I looked at my granny and said, "Yeah, but that has nothing to do with why I don't have a man, nor have a desire to date as of right now." I said.

"Baby, mama only messing with you." My mother added.

I shook my head as the three of us laughed. I loved my mother and granny dearly, however, I sometimes wondered when love would find me. True enough since Gino, over the years I dated here and there, but nothing solid enough to say that it was a true relationship. Most of these guys now of days were out playing games, which was sad. I truly understood Terry Mcmillan's book, *Waiting to Exhale*. I understood it from a now grown woman's perspective. Mannie walked back into the shop twenty minutes later looking like a brand new person, cute as a button with his fresh haircut.

"Mama, Rodrick said it's on him." Mannie said handing me the twenty dollar bill while trying to eat an ice cream cone that Rodrick probably got him from the store next door. I looked up at my mother and then at my granny to see their expressions. Both had smiles on their faces, even the damn nail tech, too.

"I don't think so. I don't mix business and pleasure." I said to the three of them.

"And how is that business for you?" My mother asked.

"Coming to your shop and patronizing mama is my business. And I just don't see Rodrick like that. And besides, he's just being nice to Mannie." I said.

"Well, he did inquire about you one time." My granny added looking at her newly polished gold nails and melodically moving side-to-side as Barry White's *Playing Your Game, Baby* played on the sound system.

"And what you tell him?" I asked wanting to know exactly what my grandmother had said.

"That you were definitely available. And as soon as he got some time to please, please, take your little old lady actin' ass out on a date." She said as my mother and the nail tech fell out laughing.

"Oh, really?" I said with an attitude.

"I'm only playing, Angie. Calm down!" My grandmother said continuing to laugh, taking out her purse to pay the nail tech.

"Uhhhmmm" I said.

I didn't think it was funny. I did not understand why they were so gun up on me getting in a relationship? I was happy being single for right now – well maybe not happy but I was content.

"Well, I am out of here. I will see you all Sunday." My granny said to me and my mother. She hugged Mannie and gave him a kiss on his cheek.

"I'll make the potato salad for Sunday dinner." I said.

"Good. Because I will be doing three pans of Glory Greens." My grandmother added which made me and my mother both burst into laughter.

"I'm serious. Jeff, Nette, and all them damn kids!" I already will be coming from church service, plus I learned my lesson the last time. Oh, hell no!" My ganny said.

The last time we all got together for a Sunday dinner, my granny made one pot of greens, once Jeff's family made their plates there were no more greens left in the pot.

"I'll be stopping at Popeye's. I already told Nette to get the deserts." My mother added.

I looked in the mirror, an hour and a half had passed and she was almost done with my head.

"Alright, Ilene I will call you later. Angie I will talk to you." My granny said as she spoke to a few other ladies that were in the shop going out the door.

I was looking forward to family dinner at my mom's Lindencrest home. After Jeff got older and married Nette, my mom sold our family home and purchased a smaller home for herself. My grandmother moved into a townhouse not too far from my mother. It was a big transition for us all but it has worked over the years.

"Mannie, you wanna go to McDonald's with granny when I finish your mother's hair?"

"Yes." He responded smiling at my mother.

Despite the rocky way Mannie came into this world, when I look back on it things really did turn out for good. Mannie is a very smart and polite kid. What I thought was my biggest mistake, turned out to be my ultimate blessing. And for that I realized that God did not punish me after all.

JEFFERY ROSHELL

IN THE DARK FILLED ROOM, ON HIS THIRD BOTTLE OF PATRON. HE SAT UP, TURNING THE LIGHT ON, AND TOOK ONE LOOK AT THE PICTURES THAT WERE HUNG AND ALIGNED NEATLY ON THE WALLS IN THE ROOM WITH HIM. FOR DAYS, MONTHS, EVEN WEEKS, PLANNING AND PLANNING WAS ALL HE DID DAY IN AND DAY OUT. COUGHING A VERY HOLLOW EVIL SOUNDING COUGH, HE STOOD UP, WENT INTO THE DIRTY BATHROOM IN THE ONE BEDROOM APARTMENT THAT HE LIVED. HE WENT INTO THE MEDICINE CABINET AND TOOK OUT THE BOTTLE OF XANAX THE DOCTOR HAD PRESCRIBED FOR THE VOICES THAT HE KEPT HEARING.

A VICTORY THAT HE HAD BEAT OUT HIS SENTENCE TO STAY IN PRISON FOR TWELVE YEARS FOR CONVICTION OF RAPE, ONLY DOING A MERE EIGHT. LIKE A CAT WITH NINE LIVES IS HOW HE BOASTFULLY THOUGHT OF HIMSELF, SMILING A VILE, WICKED SMILE. STANDING IN THE MIRROR, NOTICING THE SIGNIFICANT CHANGE THAT NINE YEARS HAD ON HIM. HE HAD PUT ON HEAVY MUSCLE MASS WHILE INCARCERATED AND SHAVED HIS HEAD COMPLETELY BALD. HIS DARK SKIN WAS NOT AS CLEAR AS IT USED TO BE, AND HIS FACE WAS FILLED WITH HAIR THAT NEEDED TO BE TRIMMED INTO A BEARD. TATTOOS WERE EVERYWHERE, INSTEAD OF THE MORRIS CHESTNUT APPEARANCE THAT HE HAD YEARS AGO, HE NOW RESEMBLED SOME SORT OF DEMONIC, EVIL SERIAL KILLER.

COUGHING AGAIN, HE CAME OUT OF THE BATHROOM, TURNED ON THE SMALL TELEVISION THAT WAS IN HIS RUNDOWN DIRTY LITTLE LIVING

ROOM. TO MUCH OF HIS SURPRISE AN INTERVIEW WAS ON WAS ON WITH A PERSON OF SPECIAL INTEREST TO HIM. HE BEGAN BREATHING HARD AS HE LISTENED TO THE VOICE, THE VOICE THAT HE REMEMBERED ALL TOO WELL. HE LOOKED UP AT HIS WALL THAT ALIGNED WITH PICTURES OF THAT SAME FACE, THE VOICE THAT TALKED ON THE TV SCREEN. HE'D BEEN FOLLOWING HER ENTIRE CAREER PATH SINCE SHE GRADUATED COLLEGE. ANYONE COULD SEE THAT IF THEY WERE TO SEE ALL OF THE PICTURES AND ARTICLES THAT LINED THE WALLS OF THE DIRTY HOLLOW APARTMENT.

GRABBING ONE OF THE PICTURES NEAREST HIM FROM THE WALL, HE LOOKED AT IT, SITTING IT DOWN IN FRONT OF HIM ON THE TABLE WHERE HE SAT IN THE LIVING ROOM. PICKING UP A RED SHARPIE, HE TOOK THE TOP OFF AND PROCEEDED TO PUT DOTS IN CERTAIN SPOTS ON HER FACE AND BODY IN THE PICTURE.

"HERE'S WHERE I WILL SLICE THE BITCH'S FACE, AND WHERE I WILL BREAK THE BITCH'S BONES." HE MUMBLED IN VOICE.

HIS CAREFUL PROJECT PLANNING, SUDDENLY TURNED INTO A RAGE OF SCRIBBLING ALL OVER THE PICTURE, AS HE CRUMBLED IT IN HIS FIST AND SLAMMING IT DOWN ON THE TABLE. HE HAD ONE AGENDA, AND ONE AGENDA ONLY. SMILING TO HIMSELF, HE THOUGHT ABOUT THE PLAN HE WAS READY TO UNRAVEL THAT TOOK A YEAR TO PLAN. KILLING CORRINE LEXINGTON WAS THE ONLY VICTORY THAT HE WANTED. HE HAD WAITED FOR THIS MOMENT FOR YEARS AS HE SAT IN PRISON, AND NOW HIS PLAN WAS ABOUT TO GO INTO ACTION. HE WAS SURE NO ONE WOULD BE ABLE TO STOP HIS PLAN.

K.J.

It was Thursday, and I decided to give Clevon a call since the last time we talked was when I was in L.A. He answered after about three rings.

"Bro, what's good?" He chirped.

"Chillin, man. Hittin' you back, I know I'm late with it and shit."

"Hell, yeah. But I figured you was busy, bro."

"How's the family?" I asked Clevon grabbing a beer out of my fridge and sitting on the couch.

"Man, everybody good. Shavela gettin' on my fuckin' nerve more and more each day. Man, it's crazy how you end up with someone that you went to school with. On top of that they're the last person you think you would end up with in school, bro. I still don't get it." Clevon said as I smirked. One thing's for sure, he was right about it. Me and Corrine could not guess for the life of us how Clevon and Shavela ended up married with kids. All they did was argue and make up, and then argue some more. I remember we had a celebration barbeque the end of last summer and we invited them both down to Miami. From the time they got off the plane, 'til the time they got back on, constant back-to-back arguing.

"First of all, if anybody is getting on anybody damn nerves it's your ass!" I heard Shavela say in the background. She was obviously listening to the conversation.

"See that's what I'm talkin' about." Clevon said to me. "Whatever!" He shouted back to her. "Anyway, K.J., how are you and Corrine?"

"We're okay. We will be in Parkersville in a few weeks for Thanksgiving." I said.

"I remembered Corrine telling me that. I just got a copy of her new book, I can't put it down." Shavela interjected. Clevon must have had me on speakerphone.

I was very happy for Corrine. With me being in the NBA Corrine could have easily fallen into that trap of just being a basketball wife and mother to Kylie. But I made sure that I always spoke of her in the interviews I did and encouraged her to be her own person outside of my shadow.

"Yeah, she's a New York Times bestselling author now." I said back to Shavela.

"Look, K.J. didn't call to talk to you, it's my convo." Clevon said irritated.

"Nigga, shut up!" Shavela replied.

"Yeah, yeah."

"Yeah, yeah my ass. See if K.J. cook you any food tonight." Shavela said cutting him off.

I just could not understand how they could do it. Hate each other every five minutes, and then you turn around and be cool. For the life of me I did not get it – hell, I did not want to get it. I was just glad that me and Corrine were far from that. I could hear Clevon taking the phone into another part of his house and closing the door.

"That's the shit I'm talkin' bout, bro. Be glad you don't have to deal with that shit!"

"Man, I'm thinking God right now." I said laughing.

"I need to come to the M.I.A. and get away from her and the kids for a few days. Shit, I need a break." Clevon said.

"Well, let me know, bro. Even though I will be there in a few weeks for Thanksgiving, if you wanna come down before I'm there." I said.

A break was something that Clevon definitely needed to clear his head. Long as I didn't have any away games he could stay for a few days and we could chill and hang out.

"Definitely. So maybe she could miss me and then beg a nigga to come home." Clevon joked.

"We all need some time away."

"Bro, I been needing it. I mean we vacation and shit when the kids get out of school for the summer. But it's mostly taking them someplace, like Wisconsin Dells or Disney World. I told Shavela even though we stay into it, we need a vacation with just us."

"Well maybe we can do something after the season is over. I say let's get together and go to Costa Rica or The Dominican Republic." I said thinking about a couples trip.

"Bro, that's wassup! I'm down." Clevon said.

"Cool, well we can start planning something once I show up in November for Thanksgiving." I said.

"Cool, bro. Like I say I'm down and this is probably what me and Shavela needs."

"Have you talked to Deon?" I asked Clevon changing the subject.

"Man, not since a week ago. You know with him being the assistant varsity basketball coach at Thornhill he and Coach Wilson are gearing up for the Thanksgiving tournament?"

"Yeah, that's one of the reasons I'm coming home for Thanksgiving. Both Thornhill and West-South are in the same Thanksgiving tournament. The other schools that are competing again are no competition from what I have seen. So they are looking at a Thornhill vs. West-South Championship Tourney game, as well as a State Championship game again." I said.

"Bro, I ain't even been keepin'. Das wassup,. You know Stanley built West-South an entire new campus?" Clevon ask which grabbed my attention quickly.

"Get the fuck out of here!"

"K.J., bro, it's nice! Looks like a small college campus, gymnasium outside made of glass. You can look inside from the outside. It's definitely that shit!"

Now this did not surprise me at all, seeing how I just donated a bunch of things to Thornhill and the media news and magazines covered it all. Stanley Brown just had to make sure I knew he was still around. He was still keeping up with me – still keeping that rivalry alive.

"I'm about to Goggle it." I said to Clevon as I opened up my Mac Laptop. I turned it on and typed in *West-South High School in Parkersville, Illinois* bringing up a picture of a beautiful state-of-the-art high school campus with a mural of a big ass panther on the side of the building.

"He got the money to do it, so good for him." I said to Clevon.

"Bro, you know his ass gotta stay relevant." Clevon chimed in.

"Lookin' to make some noise, too" I said.

"Been waitin' on the season, bro. Got some bets with a few cats at the gig. I definitely know I got some bills comin' my way and I don't mean dollars." Clevon said and I laughed.

"Well, dude, I done chopped it up wit' you enough, got some shit to go and do. Tell Shavela I said bye and I will holla at you later."

" Cool, bro. Hit my line later." Clevon said.

"Definitely will."

"Peace." Clevon stated.

"Fo' sho'." I said as I hung us the phone.

CORRINE

"Goooood morning, Miamiiiiii!!! 105.6 Miami South Radio, it's your girl, Carrrrlitha Jay!!! Bringing you today's hottest music. Well, this morning I am excited because we have the beautiful, author extraordinaire, none other than Miami's own national bestselling author and NBA wife to the fine as hell K.J. Lexington, point guard to the Miami Fahrenheit, Corrine Anderson-Lexington! Hey Corrine!!!"

"Hellooo, Miami!!!" I said into my mic that faced me in the studio. It was seven in the morning. I had just gotten a muffin and had a mug of coffee in front of me. I was not an early morning person at all. My day usually did not start until around 11:00 am, then it was just running on the treadmill in the workout room that me and K.J. had, or either tending to Kylie when Martha had to start cooking and cleaning .

"Well, we are definitely excited about having you on this morning to talk about your new book, and also your life as a basketball ball wife. So let's start by talking about this new book." Carlitha said holding up her copy that I had signed for her..

"Well, my character Mia is torn between two loves. So I wanted to really show the difference in a genuine love that she has for Blake, and a lustful, needy love that she has for Darvin."

"And I must say, I have started reading the first 50 pages and I cannot put it down! There has not been a down period so far from what I have read. I am really enjoying this book!" Carlitha said.

"Thank You!" I replied quickly taking a sip of the coffee.

"So talk to us. You are married to Miami Fahrenheit forward, number 34 K.J. Lexington. You two actually make a cute couple, I heard you guys have been together since you were fourteen-years-old?"

"Yes, since the eighth grade where we met in gym class, and it's been history for us ever since. We have had our ups and downs, even experienced a breakup in high school. But we eventually got back together. I could not have asked for a better husband and father to our daughter, Kylie Chyanne." I said smiling.

"And what a beautiful daughter you guys have."

"Thank you, again!" I replied again to Carlitha.

"So, I hear you're ten year high school class reunion is coming up next year?"

"Oh, yes! I am anticipating it. K.J. is anticipating it as well. I cannot wait to see our classmates and how they look now. I am still shocked that ten years has passed that quickly".

I was excited about the accolades I accomplished. College was a four-year breeze at U of I. I looked up and I was graduating in 2004, pledged Alpha Kappa Alpha, and even cheered the last year which K.J. and the basketball team took home the NCAA Championship Trophy. I snapped out of my thoughts when I heard

Carlitha say she was getting ready to open up the lines for a few calls before the interview was over.

"Hello, caller, you are on the morning blaze with Carlitha Jay and Corrine Anderson- Lexington!"

"OMG! Ahhhhh!!! I cannot believe that I am talking to Corrine Anderson-Lexington! My name is Kim and I have all your books! I even came to the Miami Black Author's Book Fair a few weeks ago. I could not get a picture with you because it was so many people there for you. I just want to say I love you, I love all your books, you are so pretty, and whoever does your hair hooks you up!" I smiled listening to the praise I was getting from caller Kim.

"Thank you so much for the love, Kim" I said.

"Oh you're so welcome. I'm almost finished with your latest and will be waiting patiently for your next book."

"I will be starting it right before the end of next year 2010." I said.

"Kim, do you have any last minute questions for Corrine before we take the next caller?" Carlitha asked.

"Yes, does that fine ass NBA basketball playing husband of yours have a brother, cousin, or friend?" I laughed at the comment as me and Carlitha met eyes. I was used to the women, teenage girls, and even little girls crushes that they had on K.J. - especially when they came to the basketball games, or when they would spot us out. Flocking to him more for a picture than me, it bothered me none. I got just as much attention from men whose wives or girlfriends read my books.

"Well he has no brothers, and cousins and friends are spoken for as well. Sorry." I said to Kim responding to her comment.

"Damn! Well just tell his fine ass I said hi. Kiss him for me and I will wait in anticipation for your next book!" Kim said making me feel proud about my writing.

"I sure will, Kim."

"Thank you, Kim for calling in." Carlitha said.

"No problem!" Kim said hanging up her call.

"Well, I think we got time for maybe one more call. Caller you on the morning show with Carlitha Jay and national bestselling author Corrine Anderson- Lexington. Who's this?"

Whoever was calling in there was a ton of static in the background. Carlitha made a face and kept saying, "caller, please turn your radio down so the static can fade out of your phone", but the caller wasn't listening.

"Caller? If you can hear me please turn down your radio. I am going to have to disconnect the call if you don't."

"Hello?" The deep voice said.

"Hello, caller!" Carlitha said into her mic looking at me and I looked at her back with the same puzzled ass look.

The voice was very hollow and scary sounding, the fact that they kept pausing in the call with silence was making me very nervous. Both me and Carlitha did not know what to make of this particular caller. I knew that I had gained a male audience for reading my books so I was a little at eased, but something just did not seem right.

"Caller, you're on the air with Corrine Anderson- Lexington, have you read the latest book?" Again another silent pause where they were not saying anything.

"Caller? Do you even know who Corrine Anderson- Lexington is?" Carlitha looked at me and I rolled my eyes because I was annoyed but all of a sudden we both heard "Yes". At that point something struck my interest as to who exactly this caller might be, something was rather odd with this call and I definitely could feel it now.

"If this is Clevon or Deon, y'all just wait. It's almost time for me and K.J. to come home for Thanksgiving, just wait until I see either of you two." I said laughing but immediately stopped when the silence over the air came again.

"Well, Corrine obviously it might not be them, but I hear that you and K.J.'s class reunion is coming up next year. So maybe this is someone else trying to not reveal themselves to you."

"Carlitha, who knows, but if they wanna play mystery guy, the reunion is coming soon you can tell me then." I said laughing but still kind of on the edge not knowing who this person was playing games. Let alone why they wanted to play childish games over a live radio broadcast.

"Well, we are about to wrap this up. Again Corrine, thank you for coming on this morning and talking about your new book. And let's not forget about your oh, so fine, excuse me when I compliment and say it, NBA husband for the Miami Fahranheit, K.J. Lexington. Caller, do you have any last words you would like to say to Corrine as we end the conversation with you?" Carlitha asked shaking her head glancing at me. I glanced back at her shrugging my shoulders as if I knew nothing, but felt the tiny hairs on the back of my neck stand up when we both heard, "See you soon" come over the speakers from the mystery caller.

ANGIE

"Louder!" I yell at my twenty-six member varsity cheerleading team as they practice a basic sideline cheer getting ready for the homecoming game Friday night against Mt. Fallenview High School. I definitely was not feeling them today, they were giving me dryness and this was something that a varsity cheer squad at Thornhill never possessed.

"Ladies, what is wrong? I mean are y'all not feeling it? It seems to be a funk in the air." I say standing up in the bleachers in front of them of the old main gym where we practiced during the week. They all looked at me like deers caught in headlights. I shake my head at them and smile. They were my babies, a squad composed of junior and senior girls.

"We sorry, Miss Marris." Egypt Thompson, the senior captain says as the rest of the girls laugh.

"Well this is your squad. Lead by example, Egypt" I say.

"Doesn't the foundation first start with the coach?" She replies back as I heard a few "oooohs". You could say Egypt was me and I was Coach Davis from my days of cheering on varsity at Thornhill years ago. The only main differences was that she was truly being funny and also did not have the guts to ever call me a bitch, well from what I knew about.

"Yes, but you're the captain. They feed off what you give, and let's not argue, I am not in the mood." I say laughing and the rest of the girls did, too.

"Anything for you, Madame." Egypt says. I point my finger but decided to let it go because I would be all night going back and forth with her.

"Anyway, so you ladies are performing to Beyonce's *Single Ladies* as your dance routine on Friday night. So I need for you all to kill it because the Centurionette Poms are not happy about this because it was their initial halftime performance." I say to the girls as they give me the and-so-the-fuck-what look.

" I thought they were dancing to *Steelo* by 702?" One of the girls says as others chime in with "right"!

"No, they were initially going to dance to *Ring On It*, but I talked to Mrs. Vallen and grabbed it before she could teach a routine." I say talking about the pom-pom coach.

"Well before practice ends, I want to show you ladies something from almost ten years ago since it will be my ten-year class reunion next year." I say coming down from the bleachers and grabbing the rollaway TV with the old VHS player on it. I press play showing the performance of our old varsity cheer squad did in Florida at a national competition. This performance almost always made me choke up with tears, whenever I needed a pick me up it was my go-to. It always made me happy to reminisce on my senior year, we took home second place at nationals.

"This is the varsity squad that I cheered on both my junior and senior year here at Thornhill. We took state and made it all the way to Florida and placed second. You ladies are a replica of that exact same squad now almost ten years later." I say to them as they watch in amazement at the tape. They spot me and yell "Look at Coach Marris," I smile watching as I flipped on the mat.

"Is that Corrine Anderson-Lexington that's married to NBA star Kenvarius Lexington?" Egypt asks.

"Yes, that's my best friend. She was the captain at the time" I reply.

"She is so pretty." Dalilah Thompson says and the other girls agree.

"Her man is fine!" Egypt says and the girls agree again. As I roll my eyes and shake my head as the performance comes to an end and I see us jumping up and down on the mat and the video cuts off.

"I wanted to show you girls this because I do plan on us winning state and going back to nationals this year. Your competition is, as always, sister school West-South." I say as they roll their eyes and smack their lips. "I know, I know but what's a better way to show them that you all are not bitter for coming in second place last year. Return the favor this year." I say trying to encourage them.

"Oh trust, we will return that favor!" Egypt says confidently.

"Well, if you all keep doing sideliners like y'all are today I don't know." I say looking at her and then the rest of the girls as they give me the *come on now* look.

"Just watch us!" Egypt says getting the other girls pumped up which is what I liked and why I made her captain of this varsity squad.

"CAUSE WE ARE THE CENTURIONS! THE MIGHTY! MIGHTY! CENTURIONS! RED! BLACK! AND GOLD!!! WE BAD!!!! THAT'S RIGHT!!! WE'RE THE CENTURIONS!!!!" The girls chant loud as I smile letting my mind flashed back to when me, Corrine, and the squad during our senior year would do the exact same chant. I give Egypt the nod that I was ending practice on this note. She gives new announcements and wraps up

for the day.

K.J.

I was leaving the last practice before the season started on a Friday evening. I only had one thing on my mind and that was eating. I wasn't sure if Corrine and I were going to go out to eat or if Martha had cook, either way I didn't care I just wanted to eat. I call the house and Corrine answers after two rings.

"Did Martha cook?" I ask.

"She was just about to. She had been telling me about this Haitian dish that she wanted me to taste for the last couple of weeks, why?" Corrine asks.

"Well, tell her she does not have to." I change my mind in an instant on not caring if we ate at home or when out to dinner. "Let's go out and have a night out, just me and you. We haven't done it in a while." I say feeling the smile form on her face through the phone.

"OK. I'll start to get ready!" Corrine says excitedly.

"Ai'ight!" I say hanging up the call blasting Lil' Wayne all the way to the house. Once I get home, I shower again and change into a nice fitted black shirt, blue jeans, a pair of Jordan's, Corrine had on a nice mid-length skirt and matching heels, I could tell that she had just gotten her hair done from the way it bounced on her head as she walked and her nails were done, too. We leave our bedroom and head down the stairs to leave for the evening.

"You two have a good time." Martha says as Corrine and I were leaving out the front door.

We both respond with "Thank you" as we walk to the car and get in. Martha locks the door behind us.

We ride to the South Beach Strip. There was a spot that we frequented that had a nice laid back and upscale setting. The food was also very pricey, so the only people that usually were in their were my team members or players from the Heat team, the

Dolphins, and the other local celebrities and stars that lived down here in this area. It's been a few months since we took a vacation. The last one was in Palm Springs. So we needed this alone time to spend some adult quality time together.

"So we only have about a good three weeks before we go home for Thanksgiving. I am so excited to see everyone." Corrine says sipping the glass of wine the waiter brought her.

"Came pretty quickly. Season starts next week." I say grabbing the bottle of beer that was sat in front of me taking a swig off the top of it.

"I haven't had a chance to talk with the other basketball wives now that the season is getting ready to start, but I'm sure my phone will be ringing soon".

"So how was the radio interview?" I ask her changing the subject.

"It was great, but there was one weird caller. Somebody called in and did not want to reveal themselves to me. Could not understand what that was about." Corrine says as the waiter places our food plates in front of us. I was having the steak and shrimp

platter loaded with veggies and potatoes, Corrine was eating on her

favorite shrimp and spring rice plate.

"Damn, I wonder who that was?" I ask.

"Ain't no telling who but it was really freaking me out. I mean

they would answer some of Carlitha's questions, but when she

asked them to say who they were it was like a dead silence. I even

thought it might have been Deon or Clevon playing."

"Probably so, I'll curse 'em both out when I talk to them." I

say which made her laugh.

"Does Martha know we are going to be gone for a week and a

half?" I ask.

"Well, I was hoping that we could take her with us this time."

Corrine says. Corrine really treated Martha like a second mother.

Martha rarely talks about her family and she was always lonely on

the holidays.

"I don't see the problem in it. She knows both our families and

I'm sure they would be happy to see her."

"Well I had already told my mother, I was just waiting on you to tell yours and to see what your feelings were." Corrine says. I give Corrine a look and she smiles back at me. "I love you, baby." She says.

"My mother will be just as happy to see Martha, too. It's sad that she has no immediate family, I know that the holidays can be very hard for her." I say ordering another beer.

"Which is why I told her to come with us this Thanksgiving. It makes no sense for her to go home and just sit until we come back."

"True!" I said agreeing.

"She's like family, K.J."

"Ai'ight, ai'ight!" I say giving Corrine a look. I heard her the first damn time, I had already said OK not sure why she was still trying to convince me.

"I already got the tickets!" Corrine says as I give her the *damn, really* look.

"I just figured that I knew you were going to say OK so I got her ticket as well"

"There really was no reason for you to ask me, Corrine. You already had your mind set" I say shaking my head and sipping my second beer.

"Well???" She said smiling.

"Well???" I reply mocking her. Corrine smiles at me and I just shake my head.

"OH MY, GOD! IT'S CORRINE AND KENVARIUS LEXINGTON!" A lady shouts from two tables across from us. I see her grabbing her phone which I knew she was coming to take a photo with us. Corrine starts fixing her hair and makeup.

"You never can be off point for the fans!" She says smiling as the lady made her way over excited and all.

"Hi, I'm Dorothy. I have read all your books and I watch all your games. You're my favorite point guard. My husband has your jersey! Baby, come shake K.J. Lexington's hand!" I stand up to shake hands with the guy who was a heavyset, dark skinned with a bald head who looks like he could be an old school player from back in the day. He says his name was Donald. The Dorothy lady had glasses on, a short haircut, was light-skinned and looked as if she turned heads as well back in the day.

"It's nice to meet the both of you." Corrine and I said in unison.

"You all as well. Man, thank you for the contribution to the Dade-County high schools that you made last year." The older man says.

"Baby, don't forget Corrine as well the reading programs that she started and the free books that she contributed to the women fighting Domestic Violence." The lady says and continues. "As well, as those living with HIV and the Paws Club." Corrine smiled as she listens to Dorothy name all her contributions that she participated in each year like it was her resume. I could do nothing but smile.

"K.J., man, you think we gonna get a ring this year? Fahrenheit got a lot of talent from trades this year." Donald said.

"Yes'sir ,we gonna try to bring it. We lookin' real heavy this season" I said.

"Can we get a picture with the two of you before we leave?" Dorothy asked.

"Yes, ma'am!" Corrine says as she got next to me and Dorothy got next to Walter. The waiter for both our tables took the picture with Dorothy's phone. We all smiled big, and the restaurant manager wanted a picture for the wall, we took a second one.

Once we got home it was about 10:30 pm, Martha said that she would be okay going home. I told her it was okay for her to stay in one of the guest rooms, but she insisted that she would be okay coming back bright and early Monday morning. Corrine checked on Kylie one more time, before coming to bed in our room.

After making sure Kylie was sound asleep, Corrine came into our room and went straight into the master bathroom. She soon emerged wearing a Victoria Secret's night gown on. I had on some Calvin Klein boxer brief that were having a hard containing my dick which was waking up. Corrine looked at me and laughed as my dick jumped in boxers.

"Stop laughin'." I said giving her an annoyed look as she climbed into bed and snuggled under me placing her head and hand on my bare chest.

"Sorry, but you know you be ready." She said.

"Am I not supposed to be? What else is it supposed to do when my wife comes into the room lookin' like she ready?" I asked.

"Oh, if I was ready you would know." She replied as I turned her on her back placing kissing on her neck as she giggled.

"I cannot see my life without you, Corrine." I said to her looking in her eyes.

"Me neither, big head!" She replied as we both laughed and kissed the rest of the night away.

JEFFERY ROSHELL

CORRINE

I don't know why I was stressing so much with this trip to Chicago. Well maybe because here it was only one week away and I would be back home. My mother called me to tell me that the twins would be there for dinner as well, that she was not doing any cooking but spending fifteen-hundred dollars for Dusties Soul Food in Matteson, Illinois to cater everything. I told her that Martha was coming which she was okay with. My mom loved Martha, she made for a good companion to Martha whenever we'd go down to visit. I called Angie to see what she was up to on a Sunday evening, probably watching some show or grading papers.

"Wassup, girl?" She said answering her phone.

"Just called to see what you were up to." I replied.

"Nothing. Shit, ready to be out of school for this break but I still have to be at the Thanksgiving tournament with the varsity girls."

"How's Mannie coming with his basketball league?" I asked her.

"Girl, my baby is a little beast on the court! The private junior high schools are already scouting him. Even had a few private high school scouts are sitting in the bleachers. I'm like the kid is only about to be ten years old. They need to slow it down." She said.

"Has Gino been here for any games?"

"Girl, yes! Pissed me the fuck off because every damn time he shows up to something, everybody flocks to him. I told him one time sit your ass down, you should be here just for your son." Angie said as I laughed.

"Y'all ain't never gonna get along."

"Hell-to-the-no! Mannie is our only sanity." She replied.

I had to agree with her. The only thing that kept them from going at it in a full-fledge argument was Mannie. But truth be told Angie was still in love with Gino, and she, as well as him, knew that.

"Girl, I need to find me a man or somethin' to at least have something to do on these lonely weekend nights!" She yelled. I laughed at her comment but then she told me to shut the hell up, as she was very serious about what she had just said. "Corrine, the men here in Chicago are dead! I hate to sound like some woe is me chick but seeing it now from a grown woman perspective, they are really dead here!"

"When was the last time you dated?" I asked her.

"Girl, that sorry ass nigga named Derrick that Shavela tried to hook me up with. All he wanted to do was talk about Gino. I had to stop him and ask him why was Gino the only thing that he wanted to talk about? I mean it wasn't like I married him. I dated him in high school and I got pregnant. End of fuckin story! And by the way, why are we talking about his ass again anyway?"

"And that was?" I asked referring to how long she talked to Derrick.

"Almost a year ago." She said after a five second pause.

"Well, Corrine it's not like I'm looking for it. I have Mannie and the cheerleaders. When it's time for me it will happen." Angie said.

"You might luck up at the reunion."

"With who?" She said quickly.

"You never know." I said.

"Anywayyyyyys!!!" She said in a crazy tone.

I could hear Phyllis Hyman playing in her background so I knew she was feeling it right now. "You about to slit your wrists over there?" I asked.

"Don't start, just 'cause Phyllis in the background playing don't mean I'm going through anything tonight. Fuck a sorry ass man right now, I am happy with life." She said.

"I actually can't wait until your ass get here in another week. Me and Shavela got a good girls night planned out. Gipson's is on the itinerary, too." Angie said.

She knew I loved that restaurant ever since she took me for the very first time, very expensive but the food was amazing.

"And I am looking forward to it. Glad that we are gonna be there for a week."

"Girl, yes."

"I'm bringing Martha with me."

"For what?" Angie asked.

"Well, she can keep an eye on Kylie while we are out. She's good company for my mom and K.J.'s mama - they love her. Plus, Angie, she has no family." I said.

"See that's sad. I don't know how some people can just do their people any kind of way. I love Martha she's such a nice lady." Angie said.

"I know, that's why I told K.J. I wanted her to come with us for Thanksgiving she's family."

"Girl, my mama think I'm about to be helping her and my granny cook this year." Angie said changing the subject.

"I thought your granny was the one to do all the cooking?"

"Not this Thanksgiving. Plus they both tired of Jeff, his wife, and their kids, not to mention Nette pregnant again."

"What?" I exclaimed.

"Yes. Jeff wants her to get her tubes tied. I'm so glad Mannie is all I have. And it probably will stay that way and that's fine with me." Angie said.

I shook my head at her comment. Angie could really be a trip, and go overboard with the fact that she did not have a man in her life. Like we were pushing forty years old and she just did not have anyone.

"So is she gonna do it?" I asked.

"Shit, she need to. Both her and Jeff younger than me and got too many kids. That's way too much fuckin' if you ask me." Angie said and I laughed.

"Hold on, Corrine." Angie said as I heard her tell Mannie to get ready to turn his game system off, get in the shower, put his pajamas on, and get in the bed because school would be coming in just a few hours for him. "He will be up all night playing that game." Angie said as she got back on the phone.

"Mannie, Mannie!" I said.

"Girl, you can have him he wants to come to Miami and go to K.J.'s games anyway." She said. "You know Gino only having him the entire summer is not enough. He gets him for those couple of months and then on an occasional holiday. Although I want Gino be more present, I'm dreading the day Mannie tells me he wants to go live with his father. Yeah, I don't think I'll be letting that happen." Angie said.

"You know that could be a problem, mother?" I said to her in a warning tone.

"I don't give a fuck! Even though he don't see Mannie that much, he's doing a good job from L.A. as a dad." She said. I kind of figured that Mannie or either Gino probably posed the question to her before. "Well, you just prepare yourself for that question in his teen years."

"And the answer will still be no." She stated. Anita Baker's *Same Old Love* started playing in her background, but I heard her cut it off. She probably knew I was going say something about this particular playlist that she had playing again.

"Angie, are you still in love with Gino after all these years?" I asked her.

"HELL NO!" She yelled back and I laughed.

"And why you laughing? Girl, the only thing that Gino could do for me is take care of his damn child. Ain't shit he got now that I want... Oh, and to stop lying in those interviews."

"Yeah, ok." I mumbled slightly under my breathe.

"What you say?" Angie clapped back.

"Nothin'" I said damn near tryin' not to laugh.

"Corrine, we ain't talkin' about shit,. I'll talk to you later." She said sounding very irritated. I knew I had struck a nerve but it was already close to nine her time, ten mine.

"Alrightty. Call me sometime this week." I said.

"I will." She replied and hit the end button on the phone.

HE PICKED UP THE PHONE TO DIAL OUT. EVER SINCE HE CALLED THE RADIO STATION AND HAD THE BRIEF CONVERSATION WITH CORRINE, HE FELT AN ADRENALINE RUSH TO KNOW MORE, TO BE CLOSER TO HER. TO BE IN HER PRESENCE. JUST STALKING HER BY SHOWING UP AT HER BOOK EVENTS SITTING IN THE BACK AND WATCHING HER AS SHE TALKED WAS NOT ENOUGH. HE NEEDED TO GET CLOSE UP ON HER, SO THAT SHE COULD SEE THE PAST STARE HER DEAD IN THE FACE. THIS WAS HIS NEXT GOAL BEFORE THE FINAL GO IN KILL. HE THOUGHT OF HIS NEXT PLAN, WHICH WAS A SPECIAL GIFT THAT HE WANTED TO SEND.

AS HE TALKED ON THE PHONE LISTENING TO VERY IMPORTANT AND SUBTLE INFORMATION, HE DECIDED THAT HE WASN'T SO READY YET TO LET CORRINE KNOW HE WAS BACK FOR HER. BUT AT THIS POINT HIS SPIRIT HAD ARISEN FROM THE DEAD. HE SMILED AND STARTED LAUGHING AS HE LOOKED AT THE TV INTERVIEW SHE DID DAYS AGO THAT HE TAPED. HE HAD BEEN HAVING THE RECORDING ON REPEAT FOR DAYS.

ANNOYED WITH THE PHONE CONVERSATION BECAUSE HE WAS NOT GETTING THE EXACT INFORMATION THAT HE WANTED TO EXECUTE ANOTHER PLAN, HE ENDED IT QUICKLY. HE KNEW THAT IN TIME HE WOULD BE FACE-TO-FACE WITH CORRINE, AND SHE WOULD STARE IN HORROR AND DISBELIEF. THE PAST THAT SHE THOUGHT SHE LEFT BEHIND IN THE COURT ROOM ALMOST TEN YEARS AGO.

JEFFERY ROSHELL

ANGIE

Music to my ears knowing that in less than a week, I would be on vacation for Thanksgiving break. Even though I still had to attend the three day Thanksgiving varsity boys' basketball tourney because the varsity cheerleaders were cheering, I still did not have to deal with the everyday life of classroom teaching. I could sit back, catch up on my morning shows, and get some much needed rest. I could not wait for spring break next year at the end of March. I would be in Miami at Corrine and K.J.'s the entire time sending Mannie with his dad.

Well this was my life… My son, work, cheerleading and still no man. I dated here and there, but nothing serious. I was starting to get worried because I would be knocking on thirty very soon.

"Ma, dad will be here next weekend!" Mannie said in an excited voice coming down the stairs to the living room where I was in the house.

"Well aren't we excited." I said giving him a smirk.

"Yes, when the season is going on I don't really get to see dad as much you know. I miss him a little."

I looked at him as he sat down next to me to watch TV. My heart dropped, thinking back to what Corrine said about him at some point possibly wanting to move with Gino. I could not bear to think about it, I would definitely be alone.

"Do you think you would want to move with your dad?" I knew the question was going to come off my lips but I did not think so suddenly and soon.

"But then what about you, ma?" He asked me.

I smiled and patted his curls. "I wouldn't want you to, but I just wanted to know."

"Well with the season dad is busy. Plus I would not want to leave my school, and beside all my friends are here, so I wouldn't leave you. I know you would miss me." I hugged Mannie and kissed his forehead. My evening was made.

"Go grab your coat. I need to go to Jewel for a few things and then we can hit Oberweis for some ice cream later. It's only 7:30 pm we'll still have time." I said as Mannie dashed up the steps to get his coat and shoes on.

I knew that once he heard Oberweis it was over. Mannie loved their birthday cake flavored ice cream. I decided to put off my woe is me about not having a man issues aside for a second, besides I probably just wanted something to eat anyway.

K.J.

I looked at Corrine as she slept, we were finally going home on a late afternoon flight to Chicago for the Thanksgiving weekend. Martha was seated next to her rocking Kylie who slept peacefully in her arms. So many thoughts were running through my head. The holiday tournament was going to be held at Thornhill in the new gym. Thornhills star senior point guard Ahmari Johnson was headed to Duke. I was anticipating seeing the kid's skills after seeing videos of him playing ball. He was a replica of me, his stats said it all.

West-South had an African kid by the name of Mawaldi Ofendini who was their star senior power forward. He was killing on the courts also with his hooping skills. Stanley Brown was already comparing the two kids to us from when we played when we were younger. I could not wait to see Stanley at the matchup of both schools at the tournament. This would mark nine years since we matched off against each other our senior year on the court. The Fahrenheit had a pretty good NBA conference record so far we were 5-4 this beginning season, next week we would be on the road to take on Philadelphia. Nike had called me about an upcoming shoot they wanted to do. There were also talks with my agent about Nike wanting to do a shoe for me. I was excited, music to my ears, you knew you made it in the NBA when you had your own shoe. It didn't even seem like three hours had passed when I heard the pilot come over the intercom saying we were entering O'Hare International Airport and the weather was forty-eight degrees at 3:30 pm in Chicago.

"Did I sleep the entire flight?" Corrine said looking at me and yawning.

"Yep, snoring like a bear and all." I said playfully.

"Oh whatever! We not even gonna talk about snoring, sir. The way you sounded at night."

How do I sound?" I asked.

"Like a three hundred pound man." I gave Corrine the *stop lying face* and she shook her head and looked at me like *no, nigga, I'm serious.*

Once we got off the plane and security met us at the entrance, we were greeted by shouts of my name and those that knew who Corrine was from her books. It took Corrine a little bit by surprise as we were used to them screaming for me, but now I was absolutely sharing the spotlight with my wife. Corrine waved and said her thank you's to those who declared they loved her. I shook a few hands myself. We headed for the doors to get into the BMW truck that awaited us to go to our summer home in New Lenox, Illinois. We purchased it two years ago because of all the summer travel we did back and forth from Miami to Chicago. The driver grabbed our bags from security, and put them in the back of the truck as Corrine, Martha, and Kylie got in the backseats and I got in the front passenger seat. Corrine's cell phone rings, and I hear her answer it.

"Hey, mama. Yes, we just got here on our way to the New Lenox house then we were going to make our way to see everyone."

"Tell my mother-in-law I said hey." I yelled out.

"She says hey my favorite son-in-law." Corrine said laughing at her mother who was excited hearing my voice.

"Alright, mama. Well, I will call you once we get in route to you guys. See you soon! Bye."

"Should I call my mother? Or we just showing up at her door step?" I asked thinking about it.

"Have you talked to her since we left?" Corrine asked.

"Yea, for a brief second but it wasn't long. I'll just wait to surprise her." I said looking down at my Blackberry as my coach sent out a mass text to me and the other Fahrenheit players about next week's Philadelphia game.

"Angie said that both Thornhill and West-South have one more game apiece before they play each other on Friday night." Corrine said.

"Well, I'm ready for this match up and to see Stanley Brown. That dude is really putting up some good stats overseas where he plays now." Stanley did a year in the NBA after we graduated high school, then he went to Spain where he met his model wife and plays ball.

"Yes, I cannot wait to see the new gym and the cheerleaders." Corrine added.

Once we arrived to the house in New Lenox we unpacked the suitcases. Once we felt that everything was settled, we took off to Corrine's mother's house. When we pulled up to the house her mother was already at the door.

"Mama!!!" Corrine said hugging her with Kylie in her arms. Her mother took Kylie and held her kissing her cheek. Her dad came out of the house and all hugged each other in excitement.

"Are y'all hungry?" Her mama asked.

"I am." I responded quickly as Corrine gave me a look.

"Well, come on in I can make something quick."

"Mama, we all planned to have dinner tonight at K.J.'s mother's. She told me to tell you and daddy that you all are invited. She's ordering a few boxes of pizza." Corrine said.

"Well, before we head over there my son-in-law said he's hungry. I can fry up something real quick." Corrine's mother responded to her.

"Mama, K.J. is not that hungry. You do not have to cook and he can wait until we get to his mom's." Corrine replied looking at me and shaking her head. She knew her mother would honor my wishes and cook. Her mother's cooking was the next best thing to my mothers and I wanted a home cooked meal, not any pizza.

"What time is the get together?" Corrine's mother asked.

"In about two hours." Corrine responded.

"Well, I guess that's enough time to wait. Martha don't worry about nothing this is a vacation for you as well." My mother-in-law said.

"Thank you, Nadine. I love to come and visit with you and Kathryn when Corrine and K.J. brings me along." Martha said in her Haitian accent.

"And we love when you come home, too! You're like our good girlfriend now. We have a bond because of the kids being married."

"Baby, lets come inside I'm sure Kylie is getting cold." Corrine's daddy said as everyone walked quickly into the house.

I grabbed the baby carrier out the backseat of the truck then went into the house. I sat down on the couch next to Corrine. Corrine's mother whipped up a quick little snack for me that I nibbled on and then we gathered in the living room for some quick catching up. Her mother was sitting playing with Kylie and talking to Martha. Her dad was watching TV but turned his attention to me to asking me about the season and who he thought was definitely going to the playoffs. I heard my phone playing the ringtone I had set for my mother and I answered.

"Y'all here already? Tell Nadine and Cornelius to come on the food should be here soon." My mother said. I relayed the message as Corrine's parents got up to get ready and we all headed towards my mom's house.

We all packed into our two vehicles and made our way over to see my mom. The ride wasn't too long and before we knew it we were pulling up to the house. "Heyyyyy!!!" My mother said as we all got out of the two vehicles that came in.

We all piled out of the cars and gathered on the porch one by one to hug my mother. She took the baby carrier with Kylie in it and went into the house followed by everyone else behind her. Once everyone was in the house and into the living room settled down, my mother cut on her entertainment system and told us that Walter would be back soon with the food. We all talked and caught up for thirty minutes before Walter came through the door with three extra-large pizza boxes and three boxes of Buffalo wings. He announced that he had to go back out to the car and get the three two liters of pop. I told him not to worry about and I got up to get it. After eating and letting our food digest a little, my mother pulled out a cheese cake that she had brought from the bakery. We decided to play a game of charades, which me and Corrine were killing everyone. Her mother and father took another turn as we all waited patiently for them to do their thing.

"Looks like moving." Corrine said.

"Car?" Martha chimed in as Corrine's mother and father both shook their heads and continued to demonstrate their performance.

"New!" My mother shouted and Corrine's father shook his head up and down signaling they got a correct word.

"New Car!" Corrine said and her mother and father both shouted yes! They played out clue to let us know they were getting a brand new car soon.

We moved right along to my mother and Walter. As they stood in front of everyone in the living room my mother started demonstrating rocking and crying.

"You're sad?" I asked and Walter shook his head no.

"You've hurt yourself?" Corrine's mother said and my mother shook her head no. Walter demonstrated patting and moving back and forth. Nobody was getting it, so my mother started rocking back and forth with her arms cradled.

"Crying baby?" Corrine said and my mother shook her head yes and no.

"Baby crying?" Her mother chimed in and said. My mother shook her head again yes and no and started demonstrating the patting that Walter did.

"Baby?" Martha said and my mother shook her head yes. Walter picked up a pad that had not been written on.

"Writing baby?" I said and my mother laughed and so did Walter.

"New?" Corrine's mother said and both my mother and Walter jumped up and down. I smiled until I saw my mother take her hands and rub them over her stomach.

"NEW BABY!" Martha yelled as everyone jumped up with excitement and hugged my mother and Walter.

I damn near passed out at the thought. My mother, well into her forties, is about to give birth to a baby and she was already a grandmother. "Awww, nooo!" I said as everyone laughed and my mother hugged me around the neck and kissed my cheek.

HE DID NOT KNOW WHETHER IT WAS THE
ADRENALINE RUSH OF THE FACT THAT HE WAS
STANDING AT THE DOOR OF CORRINE'S HOME. ON THE
OTHER HAND THAT HE HAD THE INFORMATION THAT
HE GOTTEN THE KEY AND CODE TO GET IN. HESITATING
FOR A FEW MORE SECONDS HE LOOKED AROUND, THEN
TOOK IT UPON HIMSELF TO TURN THE KEY IN THE
LOCK. HE HEARD THE ALARM SYSTEM BEEPING ON THE
WALL AND HE WALKED OVER TO IT TO DISARM IT.
MUSIC TO HIS EARS ONCE THE SOUND OF THE ALARM
HAD STOPPED. HE WALKED INTO THE LIVING ROOM,
THERE WAS A LARGE PAINTED PICTURE OF CORRINE
AND THAT PUNK ASS NBA NIGGA SHE MARRIED THAT

SHE HAD BEEN WITH SINCE HIGH SCHOOL. IT STOOD OUT ON THE WALL.

HE CAUGHT HIMSELF FROM ALMOST GOING OVER TO IT AND DOING DAMAGE TO IT. BEING DISCREET WAS THE WAY HE HAD TO PLAY THINGS WHILE HE WAS HERE IN THE HOUSE. WALKING TOWARDS THE STAIRWELL, HE MADE HIS WAY UP AND INTO THE MASTER BEDROOM. NOT BAD AS HE THOUGHT TO HIMSELF LOOKING AROUND. HE STARTED GOING INTO DRESSER DRAWERS WHERE HE THEN FOUND CORRINE'S UNDERWEAR DRAWER. HE PICKED UP A PAIR OF HER VICTORIA SECRET PANTIES AND SNIFFED THEM WHILE HE HELD THEM TO HIS NOSE. CLOSING HIS EYES TOOK HIM BACK TO THE NIGHT WHEN THE ALTERCATION HAPPENED AND HE DAMN NEAR GOT A CHANCE TO ROPE HER IN REAL GOOD UNTIL SHE BIT HIS DICK AND GOT AWAY. IT WAS SOMETHING HE WOULD NEVER FORGET, ESPECIALLY THE PAIN OF IT ALL.

HE PLACED THE PANTIES BACK INTO THE DRAWER AND CLOSED IT. HE WALKED OUT OF THE BEDROOM AND AROUND A FEW OTHER ROOMS, EVEN TO THE BABY'S ROOM. HE WENT IN HIS POCKET AND PULLED OUT A NOTE, WHICH HE STUCK IT WAY DEEP INTO THE BACK OF THE BABY'S DRAWER. SMILING TO HIMSELF, HE WALKED OUT, DOWN THE STAIRS, TURNED ON THE ALARM, AND KNEW HE HAD LESS THAN THIRTY SECONDS TO GET OUT AND LOCK THE DOOR BACK BEHIND HIM.

CORRINE

Surrounded by security and police me and K.J. made our way into the new main gym of Thornhill High School. The gym looked amazing! The contractors really had done a good job on the new gym. I and K.J. took seats in the visitor's section right behind the team and coaches. I looked to find Angie and she was with the varsity cheerleaders where they stood to cheer. She saw me and motioned for me to come over. I pointed to one of the body guards that I was going over to talk with her. He stood up and walked with me making sure no one got close up me. Once we got over I told him it was okay.

"Ladies, look whose here?" Angie said with excitement as the girls all screamed and hugged me in unison.

"It's me!" I said as they all laughed.

"Oh my, God!" was their response, they were in shock and awe.

"I gotta get a picture for the yearbook!" A staff member from the school said. We all huddled and took the picture. I told Angie I was going to go sit back with K.J. but I looked up and he was already talking with Clevon and Deon.

"You can always stay over here." Angie said as I sat down next to her. I saw K.J. look up at me, I smiled and mouth to him that I was going sit here for the game. He pointed that he was going be right with Deon and Clevon and the varsity boys' basketball team.

One body guard stayed near him, as the other one that was with me did the same. I pretty much figured they were going to do just that as the gym started to fill up to capacity. The announcer got on the microphone and announced the championship game for the Thornhill Thanksgiving Tournament. I saw another set of police and body guards come in as Stanley Brown made his way over to the West-South parent section and the crowd went just as wild as they did when me and K.J. came in.

"Alright, ladies!" Angie said as the twenty-seven plus varsity cheerleaders walked over to the varsity boys' team. The West-South's varsity cheerleaders did the same. I saw K.J. get up to go and speak to Stanley Brown. They man hugged each other like they were old friends that had not seen each other in years. The staff member, who apparently was a part of the yearbook committee, took a picture of K.J. and Stanley. The starting line ups were called, the jump ball was about to get underway, and the Thornhill cheerleaders stomped the floor and called out "Tip it, tip it, our way" chant. The West-South cheerleaders came with "Get it, jump up, get it, get it," and they were just as loud.

"Nothing has changed about this rivalry." Angie said to me.

"Girl, I see!" I said as number twenty-two for Thornhill Desean Smith quickly got the ball in the jump ball and sprinted to the baseline for a shot for two and it connected. Thornhill's crowd went wild and West-South's side booed a little.

Angie told me she left Mannie at her mom's because Gino was not coming home for Thanksgiving or to the tournament game. Out of nowhere I saw the kid named Mawaldi OFendini hit a three-pointer for West-South and it scored. It sent the crowd on West-South's side up in excitement, Thornhill called a time-out. West-South's cheerleaders came on to the floor did a small cheer and went back to their side of the court. It was already through the first quarter and the score was 16-13, West-South had the lead. Shavela walked in, saw me and went flying over to where we were and she hugged me.

"I told y'all I was coming." Shavela said as she looked like she had just gotten her hair done and she was in a nice jacket, blue jeans, and heels.

"Well, we knew that!" Angie said as she jumped up when Ahmari Jackson on Thornhill's team crossed over Mawaldi from West-South and connected a three into the basket. West-South called a time out, the score was now 23-27, and Thornhill was in the lead with 1:54 seconds left of the second quarter before half time. K.J. was talking with Clevon, and Deon was really coaching hard this game. I could see him in the team huddle with his play board directing different strategies and ways of getting the win. Thornhill's varsity cheerleaders started flipping down to the sidelines where West-South's cheerleaders were, and West-South's varsity cheerleaders started doing the same as both teams' crowds went wild. I could not wait to see the half-time performances. Angie told me that both squads still were good, and that Thornhill's cheerleaders were the replica of our varsity squad our senior year.

"Where y'all wanna go after the game for drinks?" Shavela asked.

"It don't matter. I'm sure K.J. gonna be with Clevon, Deon, and possibly Stanley Brown. If he decides to hang with them." I said.

"Well, I just have to call my mother and let her know that I will pick Mannie up a little later." Angie said to us as she took out her cell phone.

"Angie, I'm shocked Gino ain't here." Shavela said looking at her.

"He said he was not coming home for the Thanksgiving holiday, but he will be here for Christmas though." Angie said as she dialed on her phone and started speaking to her mother.

"And it's half-time, with the Thornhill Centurions leading with 34 and the West-South Panthers 29. Ladies and gentleman, please welcome the varsity cheerleaders from West-South High School!". The announcer stated as West-South's side went wild. There were also a few boos from the Thornhill side.

West-South's varsity cheer team now had black girls in the mix, as it was all white when me and Angie were in high school. I watched as they flipped and did different builds, jumps, and stunts, and cheered with a very powerful volume that has always been with the West-South varsity cheer team. They came off the floor and the announcer brought out the Thornhill varsity squad.

I must say that Angie really was doing a dynamic job. They were definitely a force to reckon with, they had energy, and every build, jump, and stunt they did was on point. They did a dance

routine to "Lose My Breathe" by Destiny's Child that they tore the

gym floor up with. Once their performance was over, the pom-pom

team came out to do a routine which they put their hearts into. I

saw K.J. coming over to me from going into the locker room with

Deon and the varsity team. The announcer must have notice

because he informed the crowd that me and K.J. were both in the

place as I stood up. K.J. grabbed my hand and we both waved as

the crowd clapped and cheered for us. Stanley did the same thing,

and got the same recognition. Well into the third quarter West-

South was now in the lead and Thornhill was trailing by five

points.

"Come on, Centurions!!!" Shavela and Angie both yelled.

Ahmari Johnson had possession of the ball, dribbled, and shot

to the hoop making the score for three points. Thornhill's fan

section rose up quickly with applause and cheers. West-South

called a timeout. The bands of both schools started playing, both

Thornhill and West-South's cheerleaders came out to the floor

standing in front of their sections doing a cheer. Thornhill's cheerleaders came back mid-court and flipped down to West-South's side, as West-South returned the gesture by doing the same. I smiled to myself thinking about the constant memories. The fourth quarter was getting ready to start, the Centurions had the lead by two points and the intensity was very high as the minutes were winding down to end the game.

"Shit, let's hit up Applebee's they will still be open." Angie said going into her bag for something.

"I'm with you on that." Shavela added.

West-South's side yelled in excitement as Mawaldi OFendini shot for a three and it connected to the hoop. The Thornhill cheerleaders started cheering harder. Ahmari Johnson came dribbling the ball shot his three which connected to the hoop and the Thornhill fans were back on their feet. The announcer stated that there was 2:39 seconds left of the Thanksgiving championship game. Thornhill was at 64 with West-South trailing with 59. I could see K.J. talking to Clevon like he was the assistant coach for Thornhill giving Ahmari Johnson pep talks to stay on Mawaldi and West-South's case.

"Why K.J. acting like he ain't a celebrity?" Angie asked giving him a crazy look.

"That's that Centurion pride!!!" Shavela added laughing.

I just shook my head watching him. It made me smile that he was really concerned with Thornhill winning this game. The ball was in West-South's hands as number twenty-five drove to the hoop but missed the shot. A Thornhill player rebound the ball, dribbled it down the court, and passed it off to Ahmari Johnson who shot and it connected for two points into the hoop. Thornhills fan section was going crazy as the announcer came over the P.A. system stating this was the exact state championship game that took place almost ten years ago in the March championship game. Maualdi Ofendini grabbed the rebound drove to the basket and made it. There was just 1:05 to play left in the game and Thornhill was still in the lead. I knew that K.J. was proud that the exact same thing that took place ten years ago was happening again and right now.

"You see Stanley Brown's face?" Angie asked with a smirk happily on her face.

"Girl, he lookin' like...." Shavela said.

"Like he knew this was gonna be the outcome of the game, but that Ofendini boy is really good." Angie added.

"Don't celebrate too hard just yet, they not down by much." I said. Both Angie and Shavela looked at me and laughed.

"Are you doubting the Centurion power, Corrine?" Angie asked looking at me.

"No, but y'all act like the game is over. They still got some time to play plus West-South is not trailing by much." I said as Mawaldi had the ball again for West-South, shot for the three and it connected giving Thornhill only a one point lead advantage.

"I told y'all." I said as Angie gave me an, *are you crazy did you jinx the game* look.

"Corrine, if they lose this game we blaming your ass." Shavela said with her eyes fixated on the game.

"If they lose that's on them." I said shaking my head. Were we really having this debate? I thought to myself. They knew damn well I did not want West-South to win. I just don't like to celebrate too early, you get to happy and that's how you lose games. I've seen it too many times.

A West-South player went to the hoop and tried to score but it did not go in. Ahmari from Thornhill caught the rebound, dribbled fast up the court, to the shot and made it which sent the Thornhill crowd going wild and the game was also over.

"And that ends the Thanksgiving Championship Game! The Thornhill Centurions are your 2009 Thanksgiving Tourney champs with a score of 73 and the West-South Panthers 67! Let's give both teams a round of applause!" The announcer said as Thornhill's side went crazy with cheers and praise and West-South's side continued to boo. K.J., Clevon, and the body guards started walking over toward our way.

"So ladies, what we doin' this evening?" Clevon asked looking to see if Shavela was going to answer first.

"Well, we were going to hang out for a girl's night." Angie answered for us.

"That's cool wit' us." K.J. replied.

"I'll have them back before midnight." Angie said to both K.J. and Clevon.

"Yes, please have her ass back before midnight. And she don't need but two drinks." Clevon said as Shavela turned her nose up at him and told him to shut the hell up. I looked at K.J. and smiled, he looked at me and hugged me and whispered in my ear.

"We got the win, baby, just like back then."

"Yes! Memories." I said as he kissed my forehead.

Deon came out of the locker room and talked to a few newscasters and reporters about tonight's game. It was amazing to see him as the head varsity basketball coach for Thornhill. K.J. went over to him with the body guards behind and the newscasters got the cameras on him asking questions. He motioned for me to come over and I did.

"And your lovely New York Times bestselling wife, Corrine. Hello, Corrine!" The Newscaster said to me.

"Hi." I responded back smiling.

"How does it feel to be back here were you guys met? Where K.J. was the star varsity basketball player? And it's almost time for you guys' class reunion. What are your feelings at this moment?"

I looked at her then, then into the camera, then at K.J. I smiled and said, "It's almost like the best thing in life, a dream come true."

ANGIE

I looked over at the clock as it read 7:08 am. Here it was already December and it did not even seem like Thanksgiving was that long ago. Now I would be getting ready for two weeks of Christmas break. It was Saturday, and today was also the day that I would be meeting and seeing Gino for the first time in a few months. This was all Mannie had talked about, this particular Saturday that his daddy would be here. We were meeting him for breakfast at Sierras in downtown Chicago at 9:00 am. Gino called to say that he had already made it here on the plane. He was staying at some hotel not too far from the upscale restaurant in the Gold Coast.

I pushed the covers back, walked into my bathroom, washed my face, and decided to get my clothes together for what I was going to wear for today. I selected my long black boots with the heels, a pair of blue jeans, and a black sweater with gold belt that went around the waist of it. I had micro braids in my head, thanks to my mother from last weekend. So all I did was put them into a pony tail, selected my gold hoops for earrings. After getting my clothes together I decided on a bath which lasted for forty-five minutes. I relaxed and soaked while I listened to old school slow R&B jams. Once I finished and got myself together Mannie was already ready playing on his game system.

"Alright, sir, let's go. Your dad will be waiting for us soon." I said to him as I came into his room and stood in the doorway looking at him.

Mannie turned the game off, got out the pair of Jordan's that he wanted to wear today, his coat and hat, and was ready to go. "Where we goin'?" He asked me looking innocent when he spoke.

"Sierras, downtown." I answered him as he replied, "yes!" He put on his coat and hat quick.

125

I shook my head, grabbed my purse and keys, opened the door so that Mannie could go out . I turned on the alarm, and closed both doors behind me locking them. I got in on the driver's side and turned on 107.5 WGCI as I cruised down the street to jump on I57-North that would lead towards downtown. My phone rang, I looked at the Blackberry screen and it said my grandmother, I answered.

"Yeah, granny." I said changing lanes on the interstate.

"Angie, what you doin'?" she asked.

"On my way with Mannie to have breakfast with Gino. He's here for Christmas break."

"Hey, great-granny." Mannie said.

"Hey, my sugar dumplin'! How's my handsome man?"

"Fine." He replied and I smiled.

"Good, you gotta come see me soon."

"I will." Mannie said.

"Okay." My granny replied ending her conversation with Mannie and bringing it back to me.

"Well I called because I kinda met someone I think might be a potential date for you." I damn near almost hit the car on the side of me. I shook my head because my grandmother and mother were constantly trying to hook me up with someone every time they felt I was becoming single for a long period of time.

I did not understand it, and hell it even got on my nerves. I had told them time and time again that right now I just was not ready to date anyone at the moment. My mother's response was always a rebuttal of when I was going to be ready. She felt that no man was going to fall out of the sky and come to marry me. I understood what my mother meant, but the furthest thing from my mind at this point was a damn man. I did not want to think about anyone that they were trying to hook me up with. I concluded in my heart that when I was ready to date I would again.

"Granny, what have I asked you and mama time and time again?"

"Angie, baby and I understand, but listen you cannot expect it to just show up at your doorstep or come falling out of the sky."

"It?" I asked her.

"It, being a man. You need to start dating, baby. You cannot bottle yourself up and cut the world off. You been like this since Mannie was born. Tell me something? When was the last time you had a date?"

I thought about the question, it really had been quite some time since I had an actual date. After the guy Shavela had hooked me up with, there was this one guy named Corey, he had a good job, nice place, thirty-one years old, worked out, and drove a Buick truck. Everything was good until Corey neglected to tell me that he was not quite over his ex. We were dating heavy for five months and one day he decided to sit me down to tell that he did not know where he wanted to go with things. He told me he didn't want to play games and lead me on. I told him to do what was best for him, got up for the table, walking out of the restaurant to my car. I never looked at any guy the same since. So here I am, twenty-seven about to be twenty-eight years old in January of the next year - no man, no ring, no white picket fence around my house with a dog, but a child, a teaching job, head cheerleading coach, but still no man fits into the equation.

"Well, Granny when it's time…"

"And when do you think that will be?"

"Granny, I don't know, but I'm not looking for it." I replied getting off the interstate turning towards Taylor Street downtown.

"Well, I think this guy would be nice for you. He's your age, not married, no kids. And from what I can tell he works out and keeps himself up, and I know for a fact that he's your type."

"How you know all this?" I said excitedly.

"I know what your type is Angie, but listen you enjoy your time with Mannie and Gino. Don't wanna do too much talkin'." She said which meant she was going to save this conversation for later because it was not for Mannie's ears to hear.

"Alright, I'll call you back later but not about that." I said quickly.

129

"Uh-huh, bye, Mannie." My grandmother yelled out.

"Bye, great nana." He replied.

I told him to hit end on the phone and he did. We rode in silence for a minute before I broke it. "I know you're excited about seeing your dad."

"Yeah, but mom I think you should start dating, too."

I damn near ran off the road. I got to the stop light and looked at him. "What did you say?" I asked him.

"That you should start dating. Mom, you should go out sometime. It's okay, I'm a big boy but I understand that you have a life, too." I smiled as the light turned green and I continued to drive.

"And where is this coming from?"

"Ma, I would like to see you happy. I really wish dad and you would be together so we could be a family sometimes." He said as I damn near teared up.

This little boy was barely ten years old but spoke like a teenaged kid. I pretty much figured Mannie had been feeling this way, but to hear him say it gave me confirmation. There were times that I wondered what life would have truly been like had things went the way they were supposed to. Truth be told I still had trouble with the fact that I did not have a husband and at least two kids at this point in my life. But with the way things were going with relationships nowadays, most people were not even considering marriage until they were in their thirties. I just did not want to end up as one of those women with one child, no man, and still searching and damn near about to hit forty.

I got off the expressway and onto Michigan Avenue. Mannie was listening to music on his iPod, which let me know that the conversation had definitely come to an end. I pulled up to the parking lot to meet the valet. A white guy who looked to be in his mid-fifties or maybe sixties came to the driver side window with a smile as big as the Grand Canyon. I grabbed my purse and phone, told Mannie to get out and come around to my side which he did, as I got out and handed the valet my keys. He smiled and told me I was very pretty. I blushed at his gesture and Mannie and I walked

to the front door of the restaurant. Once inside, I told the maître d

we were here for a reservation and he immediately took us to a

private booth area that Gino had reserved. He was looking good

with his hair cut, beard and mustache trimmed, and groomed

neatly. He was wearing blue jeans, gym shoes, and a nice sweater.

"Dad!" Mannie said with excitement as him and Gino

embraced each other with Gino lifting him up off the ground and

kissing him on the cheek. I smiled as Gino put Mannie back down

and gave me a two second hug, which we both sat down facing

each other as Mannie sat opposite next to me.

"How have you been Angela?" Gino said calling for the waiter

to come over as he sipped a bottle of Heineken beer.

"Great, Gino." I replied telling Mannie to order so I could after

him.

"Good. I'm glad to have been off to meet with you and

Mannie. I also came home to visit my family which I want to take

Mannie to see them with me today." Gino said.

"Okay." I said sipping the mimosa that I ordered.

"I have not talked to your mom in a while. How is she doing?" I asked him as a plate of small sausages wrapped in pancakes, with three small cups of syrup was sat down in front of us, and Mannie dug into it quickly.

"She's doing good. She told me that she had not seen Mannie in a while which is why I wanted to take him by there." Gino said.

"Yeah, I've been so busy with everything from cheerleading to grades and the students." Gino shook his head as he grabbed a small plate and started to get some of the spinach dip as well. I looked at his hands just to see if they were manicured, and they were. He had nice and neat hands and fingers like he'd really been taking care of himself and he was wearing CK One for men. Damn, I thought as he was looking really good even though he made me sick this last ten years.

"I wanted to talk to you about something. I know you may not want to hear this, but I was thinking about Mannie possibly coming to live with me for a year." Gino said as I gave him *the hell he will* look.

"Gino, Mannie is not coming to live with you anytime soon." I said lowering my eyes at him picking back up the mimosa glass.

"Well, he needs a father figure in life, especially now that he is getting up there in his teenage years. Not saying that you have not done a good job with our son, but he's at that age Angie where he is going to need a father figure in his life. Before you know it he will be almost twelve."

I looked at Gino and laughed. Mannie caught my gesture and shook his head as he was ready to hear what was about to come out of my mouth, which was not going to be nice at all.

"I hear you loud and clear, Gino, but Mannie is not coming to live with you." I said as our meals were sat down in front of us by the waiter. I ordered a veggie omelet, Mannie had bacon and scrambled cheese eggs with white toast, and Gino had a steak egg and cheese skillet.

"Why is that?" Gino asked with a look of disgust.

"Because I think it is more befitting for him to live with his mother, and to have the regular summer break visits with you. Besides you're an NBA player, how would you have time to spend with him while you're on the road?" I said to him blinking and waiting for a response.

"Just like you work and cannot spend every moment with him, I would do the same."

"That is not the same, Gino. You will be away on the road not really spending time with Mannie. I just do not see your logic as to why he should come and live with you." I said cutting him off and ordering another drink.

This motherfucker had the nerve to want to have this as a conversation piece. I was not having it, not now, not never. And it was not that I just did not want Mannie to go, I just didn't want Mannie to be neglected just to help Gino with his ego and guilt.

"Well, I think it's something that we should revisit soon. I really am thinking about wanting to have him live with me once he's out of junior high school." Gino said.

I took another sip of the mimosa, looked Gino dead in the eyes, and with every syllable mouthed, "I said, no!"

"Look! I'm the boy's damn father, too!" Gino shouted as the waiter interrupted us both by asking if we were okay. He even had the nerve to ask that we please keep it down the other guests in the restaurant were starting to stare.

We both looked at him and I continued our conversation. "That has nothing to do with the fact that it would be best for him to move and live with you." I said a little heated that he had raised his voice at me. Gino could tell that I had the upper hand as he chose to be quiet and eat his food. He was just as heated as I was and I did not give one good damn about it.

"Mannie, what do you think about living with me?" Gino asked him smiling turning his attention on him. I laid my fork down waiting to hear this response.

"I don't know, dad. I mean I love living with mom. I love it here in Chicago, to move to California with you? I would miss mom." Mannie said.

I smiled knowing I definitely had won this battle. If he thought for one minute that he was going to win this one, he really had bumped his damn head somewhere.

"Well, I really would love for you to come and live with me so you can meet Krista and your soon to be here baby brother."

Mannie and I both looked at Gino and said, "Huh" in unison.

Gino smiled sipping the third Heineken he had ordered from the bar. I looked at him like a deer in headlights as I heard Mannie yell, "Cool, I'm gonna be a big brother!"

It's as if I felt like I was at his dinner table with his parents and ex-girlfriend all over again nine years ago. Taking the last sip of my mimosa, I shook my head as we locked eyes. Gino looked for me to respond, but all I could do was order another glass from the bar.

K.J.

"Baby, I'm so glad we won tonight!" I said to Corrine as we came in the house from the Fahrenheit and New York Knicks Game. I had a total score of twenty-one points, seven assists, and twelve rebounds.

"Yeah, it was a good game! I just can't believe it's a few weeks from Christmas and the New Year." She said taking Kylie from Martha after she laid her purse on the counter and sanitized her hands.

"Yep, I figured we would take New Year's Eve day spending it in the Bahamas?" I said smiling as I watched her face light up. I knew she had wanted to go for a while now, and I was trying not let the cat out the bag, but it kind of slipped.

"Nice, bae! I have to get started on my next novel as soon as we come back. Brenda called last week reminding me that my break was coming to an end soon." She said sitting down on the couch with Kylie.

" I still cannot believe my mother is pregnant."

"Why? She's still in her early forties, K.J." Corrine said looking at me.

"I don't know, but it's gonna be so awkward. Kylie being older then her aunt or uncle."

"Yeah, but it's people that have grandkids and still have kids now because they had their kids very early. Look at Angie and her mother and grandmother, prime example."

I guess I could see the logic behind it, but damn I was pushing thirty soon, and my mother was about to have another kid. It was really hard for me to wrap my head around it.

"Have you talked to your mother since last week?" Corrine asked.

"Naw, I'll call her tomorrow." I said going up the staircase.

I left Corrine to talk with Martha and watch TV. I opened the master bedroom door and decided to unwind and put on some shorts and a tank top. I figured I would go out on the patio and have a cigar and just watch the moonlight. Looking off into the distance of the Miami night life, I dozed off thinking about all the accomplishments that I have achieved since college, and even high school. I heard my cell phone ring, looking at the screen it said "Dad" going across, I answered it. "Hello." I said putting it on speakerphone sitting it down on the ledge next to me.

"Son, how are you?"

"Good, dad, and you?"

"Can't complain. I saw that New York Knicks game tonight, y'all kicked ass."

"Yeah. It was an easy win, all over the boards with points. We play the Celtics after the new year." I said as Corrine came out to the patio and I told her it was my dad. She told me to tell him hi, which I did.

"So I heard your mother let that nigga knock her up." My dad said laughing.

"Yea, can't believe it either. I had to ask her why she waited so late in the game to get pregnant again. Even though she is in her early, middle forties." I said seeing Corrine give me the evil look at how I was talking about my mother to my dad.

"Especially with Kylie being the grandbaby, now. Kylie is going to be an older niece."

"Yeah." I said wanting to change the subject.

"How is everyone?" I asked.

"Doing good, son. Everyone is doing good. We just ready for the holiday and the new year to come in."

"Yeah, my ten year is next year."

"Son, it don't even seem like you've been out of school ten years." My dad said.

"I remember just walking across the stage yesterday, dad. Time is flying."

"That's for sure."

"You comin' up anytime soon?" I asked him coming back into the house with Corrine behind me as she shut and locked the patio ledge door.

"I've been thinkin' about it, but it won't be until after the snow and all. New Jersey still has them Chicago winters. And hell, if I could find a decent job, I would move down there to Florida with you all today."

"You could always start lookin' now." I said.

"True. I just might, son." My dad replied.

I was happy that our relationship was better than what it was when I was a growing up. My dad and my mom divorced when I was a young teenager, and my mom moved me and her to Chicago from New Jersey. My dad was still in Jersey most of childhood, so my uncle, my mom's brother, was more instrumental in my upbringing. Even though my dad still tried to be in my life, part of me resented him because he moved on so quickly by starting another family. I felt that he didn't even try to work things out with my mother. It took me a while to forgive him, but I did.

"Well let me know if I can help, dad."

"Son, you just work on playin' in the NBA. I will take care of that." He replied.

I looked at my phone and it was a text message from Deon. He was saying that he and Shavela were coming on a surprise visit to Miami for the New Year to spend it with me and Corrine. I smiled and texted back, "Come On." What better way for us to bring the New Year in than with the two of them.

My dad said that he had to go and make a few quick runs before his night ended. I told him that I would talk with him soon, he replied the same as we both ended the call.

CORRINE

I walked out of the room and grabbed Kylie from Martha. It was time for me to lay her down and put her to sleep, it was passed her bedtime. I had a very eventful day, the basketball wives for the Miami Fahrenheit were having a get together in about three weeks where we would discuss some of the upcoming meetings for the new year. As always I was really excited about this because I spear-headed most of these events. I enjoyed the fact that the ladies made me in charge of things. I always had some special things going on for the basketball husbands that the wives would put together.

I gave Kylie a bath in her little tub, shampooed her hair, put baby lotion her body, got her dressed, and gave her a bottle. After playing baby lullabies that finally knocked her out in my arms, I kissed her cheek, and walked her to her crib in her room. First, cutting on the baby monitor that was in her room, I pulled her little covers back in the crib and laid her in position, she let out a cooing sound and a yawned.

"Goodnight, fat mama." I said to her. Laying her back I noticed that something was on the side of her cover that I had not seen before. It looked like some sort of picture. I reached for it and noticed that it was turned the opposite way. I made a face as I turned it around. I thought my eyes were playing tricks on me. My hands trembled and I let out the loudest scream that sent Kylie into a raging fit waking her up out of her sleep.

K.J. and Martha both rushed into the room to see what was going on. I dropped the photo on the ground still looking at it as my hands and lips trembled hearing both K.J. and Martha ask me what was wrong, but I was in too much shock to even speak a word.

CLASS REUNION

IRRITATED ONCE AGAIN BY THE CALL THAT HE PLACED. NOT BEING ABLE TO GET ANYWHERE OR ANY PROGRESS ON THE INFORMATION THAT HE NEEDED TO MAKE HIS MOVE. HE DECIDED TO LET THE CAT OUT THE BAG.

"YEA, I WAS THERE WHILE EVERYONE WAS AWAY ON VACATION LAST MONTH. AND DON'T WORRY ABOUT HOW I GOT THE DOOR CODE. IF I WANNA WALK UP IN THERE NOW AND KILL UP EVERYONE I COULD." HE SAID WITH VILE IN HIS VOICE.

"LISTEN, THIS BITCH SENT ME TO PRISON. SHE DOES NOT DESERVE TO LIVE, NOT TO HAVE A LIFE. CORRINE

WILL ANSWER TO ME FACE-TO-FACE SOON AND THERE IS NOTHIN' THAT ANYONE CAN DO ABOUT IT! YOU CAN TRY TO WARN THE AUTHORITIES I WILL JUST MOVE AROUND. REMEMBER I'M OFF ON GOOD FAITH FROM THE SYSTEM. NOT SITTING AT HOME ON A MONITOR. SO IF I WANTED TO GO BACK TO CHICAGO AND RELOCATE I COULD."

THE CONVERSATION WAS REALLY PISSING HIM OFF. TO THINK THAT HIS OWN FLESH AND BLOOD WOULD NOT SIDE WITH HIM ON THE SITUATION. FAMILY WAS SUPPOSED TO BE EVERYTHING. HOW COULD THE WOMAN THAT BIRTHED HIM NOT WANT TO HELP OUT? SHE HAD NO IDEA THAT YEARS LATER, HER BEING IN HAITI, BUT COMING TO MIAMI WOULD HAVE FATE FOR HER TO BECOME THE HOUSEKEEPER OF CORRINE ANDERSON-LEXINGTON. THE WOMAN THAT SENT HER ONLY SON TO PRISON FOR NEARLY RAPING AND BEATING HER AND OTHER WOMEN. HIS MOTHER

REALLY HAD NO RELATIONSHIP WITH HIM WHEN HE
LEFT MIAMI FOR ILLINOIS AS A YOUNG MAN.

HIS MOTHER COULD NO LONGER DEAL WITH HIM,
HE WAS A TROUBLED CHILD AND NEEDED A MAN TO
GUIDE HIM IN THE RIGHT DIRECTION OF LIFE. BEING
RAISED BY HIS DAD WHO WAS JUST AS MESSED UP IN
THE HEAD AS HIM, ONLY MADE SENSE AS TO WHY HE
DID WHAT HE DID. HE USED WOMEN, THEY WERE A
TOY, MERE NOTHINGS. TEASED BY THEM IN HIGH
SCHOOL, CALLED ALL TYPES OF NAMES BECAUSE OF
HIS APPEARANCE, NOT BEING ATTRACTIVE AT ALL
DURING HIS SCHOOL DAYS. THE ONE RELATIONSHIP
THAT HE HAD, BEING PLAYED AND USED, FOR THE
ENTIRE SCHOOL TO FIND OUT AND MAKE A MOCKERY
OF HIM. IT WAS AT THAT POINT IN HIS LIFE, HE WOULD
NEVER PLAY GAMES WITH A WOMAN AGAIN!

HE CHANGED HIS APPEARANCE GETTING INTO
SHAPE AND TURNING 289 POUNDS OF FAT INTO A SLIM
198 POUND FRAME. HIS WAY OF THINKING CHANGED,

WOMEN ADORED HIM, RESPECTED HIM, AND WANTED HIM. HE WENT TO COLLEGE AND EARNED A COMMUNICATION DEGREE SETTING THE BAR FOR HIS ARTICULATION. AND THE WAY HE WAS ABLE TO SMOOTH TALK AND NEGOTIATE ANY GIVEN SITUATION.

HIS FIRST VICTIM TEASED HIM, AND TEASED HIM, UNTIL THE NIGHT HE GOT HER TO HIS APARTMENT IN THE FLOYD HOME PROJECTS OF PARKERSVILLE. SHE REALLY THOUGHT HER REPEATING ACTS WERE GOING TO TAKE PLACE AGAIN THAT NIGHT AT HIS PLACE. HOW WRONG SHE WAS AS HE COULD TAKE NO MORE, HE CUT THE MUSIC UP, DRAGGING HER AROUND HIS APARTMENT BEATING HER LIKE A CHILD WHOSE TEACHER HAD TO CALL HIM AT HIS JOB BECAUSE SHE WOULD NOT STOP ACTING UP IN SCHOOL. NO ONE COULD HEAR HER SCREAMS AS HIS RAGE INCREASED AND INCREASED. SHE HAD NO FAMILY THAT CARED

FOR HER. NO OLDER BROTHERS OR UNCLES. HE HAD DONE HIS HOMEWORK BEFORE MAKING THIS MOVE.

SHE WAS A BLOODY MESS IN THE FACE AND SCREAMED THAT SHE COULD BARELY HEAR ANYTHING. HE PUT HIS .38 TO HER HEAD AND TOLD HER IF SHE TOLD A SOUL HE WOULD KILL HER MOTHER WHO WAS WELL-KNOWN IN THE COMMUNITY. HE DROPPED HER OFF A BLOCK FROM THE HOSPITAL WHERE SHE WOULD WALK THERE AND TELL THEM THAT SHE WAS ROBBED AND BEATEN WHEN SHE GOT INTO THE ER. SHE DID EXACTLY WHAT HE HAD TOLD HER TO DO, NEVER SPEAKING TO HIM AGAIN OR MAKING CONTACT. AFTER THE FIRST, THERE WERE OTHERS WHO EXPERIENCED THE SAME WRATH, SAME SCENARIO NEVER GOING TO THE COPS ABOUT ANYTHING. UNTIL HE MET CORRINE, WHO DID THE EXACT OPPOSITE AS SHE HAD GOTTEN AWAY THAT NIGHT BEFORE HE COULD REALLY DO DAMAGE. NOT ONLY WAS THIS BLOOD BOILING ON HIS END, SHE WAS

SAVED BY HER BOYFRIEND AT THE TIME WHOM THE BITCH ENDED UP MARRYING AND HAVING A HAPPILY-EVER-AFTER LIFE. WHILE HE WAS SENT TO PRISON AS SHE TESTIFIED AND THE OTHERS CAME FORTH FROM HIS PAST AND DID THE SAME. IT WAS AT THAT MOMENT WHEN HE LOOKED AT HER AS THEY WERE TAKING HIM AWAY IN THE COURTROOM, CORRINE WOULD PAY FOR WHAT SHE HAD DONE.

"I'M NOT GOING TO STOP AND YOU OR NO ONE ELSE CAN STOP ME. SHE WILL PAY FOR WHAT SHE HAS PUT ME THROUGH THESE PAST YEARS! I HAVE A SCORE TO SETTLE. HER BLOOD ON MY HANDS IS WHAT I WANT!"

NOT LISTENING TO HIS MOTHER HE HEARD HER RAMBLE ON-AND-ON-AND-ON, TELLING HIM TO STAY AS FAR AWAY FROM THE HOME SHE WORKED AT AND CORRINE AND HER FAMILY. MORE HIS MOTHER TRIED TO TALK HIM OUT OF DOING ANY HARM THE MORE ANNOYED WITH THE CONVERSATION HE WAS. JUST AS HE WAS GETTING READY TO HANG UP LIKE HE

NORMALLY WOULD HE HEARD THE SOUND OF A FEMALE'S SCREAM FROM HIS MOTHER'S END OF THE PHONE. HEARING CORRINE SCREAM SENT A GRIN THE SIZE OF THE GRAND CANYON ACROSS HIS EVIL FACE. AT THAT MOMENT HE KNEW HIS FIRST MISSION IN HIS PROJECT HAD DEFINITELY BEEN ACCOMPLISHED.

2010

CORRINE

I admired the fifteen-thousand dollar oil painting that was just placed on the living room wall of my house for the second time. It was me, K.J., and Kylie. The painting was all three of us dressed up for an NBA Awards Gala that K.J. was honored at here in Miami last year.

"I love this painting, Mrs. Lexington." Martha said standing next to me. We both were just amazed at how elegant and prestigious it looked.

"It's very nice, Miss Martha." I added.

154

"Well, I have finished preparing dinner for you all. Baked chicken spiced with red and green peppers, Spanish rice, and my famous cornbread." I could feel my stomach muscles work listening to Martha talk about what she prepared for dinner, that cornbread that she made in the muffin tray was to die for. She would not tell me what she put in it, but it was good. I walked up the stairs to the master bed room towards the patio door opening it. I let my hair flow with the February wind. It was 6:00 pm and K.J. was due home from his away game in Texas any minute. Kylie had a bottle, knocked out early, and I was just in my thoughts. Looking out into the Miami downtown skyline, my mind drifted a month or so back. A chill started to come up my back, for the life of me I could not understand how that picture of him got into Kylie's crib. It took me back to a time that I had put behind me years ago, but also brought me to the last time I saw him and the look that he had given me. A very scary smirk on his face as they took him out of the courtroom where I stood trial against him for what he had done to me and other girls in the past. Martha said that she had found the picture cleaning, and by mistake instead of giving it to me she left it in between Kylie's sheets the night before. Martha did ask me

who he was in the picture. I told her that I'll tell her all about it one

day when I felt comfortable. Even though he was so behind me,

just seeing his face in that picture after all these years sent a feeling

of uneasiness through my body. I jumped as I felt K.J. rubbing my

shoulders bringing me back to reality from my jilted thoughts.

"You okay?" He asked me hugging me from behind.

"Yea." I responded as we both looked up at the sky.

"How's the new book comin'?"

"It's comin', just drawing up an outline and characters right

now." I said. I loved the fact that K.J. was just as much concerned

with my career in writing as his own playing basketball on the

court.

"Take your time, baby. You can do it I'm so proud of you."

"Thank you." I smiled as he snuggled and held me a little

closer. I felt a sense of closure and protection. The thoughts of him

as I referred to Marcus were suddenly gone, he was far away in prison. So tonight I would put it all behind me, it was done, no

more worrying, life would go on and the past was to be just that.

ANGIE

"Oh, really!" My mother shouted loudly over the sound system at her shop. I was there getting my hair and nails done.

"Yes, but I told him that he can forget it thinking that Mannie is gonna come and live with him. And then he announced that he's seeing someone and she's expecting." I said with much attitude in my voice.

"Fuck it." My mother said as she curled a ladies head. *Love Angel* by JS came over the sound system and I heard a few, "That's my song" from the ladies who were in the shop.

"Oh, I'm over it." I told my mother referring back to the conversation.

"You sure about that?" My mother asked giving me the eye.

"And why would you ask me that?" I replied back.

"Well, for one the way you talk about Gino I still feel like you carrying hurt, baby. And you need to let it go." My mother said.

I looked at her and made a face. Me still in love with Gino? Yeah right. He could have showed up with the girl for all I gave a damn. "Ma, I'm so over Gino it ain't even funny. I don't know what would ever make you think something like that."

"Baby, I know. You can play that role with somebody else but you talkin' to your mama here! I birthed you, and you a woman just like me. When a man does wrong and we still have feelings for him we show every emotion of hate before we can simply let go. And Angie you have not let go, yet. It's understandable but you need to tell yourself that." My mother said. I looked at her and laughed, almost getting burned by the flattening curler that was being applied to my hair. "Like I said when you can come to grips with it, you will move on with life."

"I have." I said.

"Okay, Ang'."

I was not about to argue with my mother this morning about Gino. I tried to change the subject as fast as I could. "Gino's not gonna be able to take Mannie for spring break and you know I'm going to Corrine and K.J.'s."

Before I could get the question out my mother replied, "Of course I will watch him for the week." I smiled.

"I'm shocked you have not asked Corrine to have K.J. hook you up with one of his team mates."

"Why would I do that?" I said back to my mother turning up my face.

"What do you mean? Let my best friend's husband play for the NBA, and I don't asked to be hooked up with any single teammate." My mother said.

I turned so she could finish my hair, but little did my mother know that Corrine actually did try at one time to hook me up with one of K.J.'s team members. It was going okay, I was actually going to introduce Mannie and my family to him, until I found out he was seeing some other girl in Mexico. She found my number, sent me a bunch of pictures and text messages to make sure that I really knew he was with her, not to mention she told me that if I wanted to continue seeing him I could, but her ass wasn't going anywhere. I ended it rather quickly and blocked him from contacting me. I never told Corrine or K.J. about it because it was not their problem or issue. I could not understand for the life of me what was up with this generation of men and dating? Was the old time way of traditional dating then marriage going out of style? I did not want to be known as a baby mama for the rest of my life, but I would rather be by myself and alone than with someone who was doing me wrong anyway.

"Well, I'm just gonna tell you and granny, don't hold your breathe. While y'all waitin' on me just be happy with who y'all got." I said with a smile.

"Oh, baby doll, I am. We're going to Red Lobster and the show tonight all on him." My mother said slapping fives with Nedra who was doing my hair but sat the straightening iron down to do so. My hair was flattened just like I loved Nedra to do it. I gave her a hundred dollar bill for the service.

"And I ain't mad." I said getting up and going over to the nail table. Tracy, the nail tech, was waiting on me.

I saw my mother grabbing her purse after finishing her client's head. The lady paid my mother, as she went to grab her coat and purse, said her goodbyes to a women she knew and left out. My mother did the same right behind the lady.

"Where you off too?" I said to her looking at the clock as it read 4:50 pm.

"To get ready for my date tonight. I need to relax and sit in the tub, and then find me a nice outfit." She said with a smirk on her face like a kid at the candy store.

"Well, have fun. Call me later." I said as I watched her walk towards the door.

"Don't wait on it." Was her reply back.

JEFFERY ROSHELL

K.J.

I was in Chicago for the night game against the Bulls. I decided

to take my mother out for lunch. I had not seen her since

Thanksgiving and she was starting to show a little bit. I was

starting to somewhat accept that my mother was pregnant, but still

trying to register that it was at such an older age of her life. Well, I

guess I would never be the only child on her side as well.

"Have you and Walter decided on names?"

"No, not yet, but I have to figure out what I am having first. I

won't know until next month." My mother said with a smile as the

waitress sat a glass of water with a lime on the side and a straw

down in front of her.

"I always wanted a little sister." I said dipping a French fry into the ketchup that sat it in front of me on the plate.

"We are actually gunning for a girl, but Walter kinda thinks it might be a boy."

"Well whatever, I am ready to be a big brother, but Kylie will have a young uncle." I said as we both laughed and nodded our heads.

"I'm just glad that you're accepting to it, I know it was kinda late for my K.J., but I didn't meet Walter until later. He's a good guy, and I would not have asked God for a better husband than the one I have now." She said speaking proudly of him.

"Well, it took a second, ma. I mean you're almost a senior citizen." I said and she gave me the look of a frown which I matched with a smile.

"Whatever! I heard your daddy had something to say and I cursed his ass out, too."

"He called you?" I asked her getting ready to eat the Rueben sandwich that was also brought to the table for me, along with my mother's chicken sesame salad.

"Yeah, I told him to worry about himself in a playful way, but he tried to be funny sayin' them *eggs still workin'*?" She said and I couldn't help but laugh. "I wanted to say so bad, that old lookin' ass wife of yours. You don't know if she is your kids actual mama, or their granny!"

I could do nothing but fall out in laughter at that point. My mother was off the chain with come backs, I believe I inherited that from her side.

"Yeah, I sure did tell his black behind that, lookin' like Sophia when she got out of jail. He, he, he, he." My mother said mocking Oprah Winfrey's character in *The Color Purple*.

"Ma, you did not tell pop that?"

"I sure in the hell did." She said sipping her water.

I shook my head. My mother and father still could playfully go at it despite the divorce that happened when I was a young kid. I was happy that their relationship was like it was now. Of course my mother would never say that to my stepmom, they both got along and the same thing with Walter, my father had the utmost respect for him.

"I couldn't ask for better parents." I said biting into the other part of my sandwich.

"Who else would you want as parents? Me and your daddy get along just fine now that we are not together. I like him a lot better than when I was his wife."

"What's the difference?" I asked her.

"Well, I don't have to put up with who he really is now that I know how he can be. Not saying that he is doing the exact same with your stepmom that he did with me, but we could never get along and see eye-to-eye. I really have understood the saying over these years. Some people are just better off friends than lovers. I mean we were married for twelve years, but your daddy could never agree on anything with me. But now that we are not together, and are on a friendship level, I can laugh and talk to him and the feelings that I had before and once the divorce was final are all gone."

I guess you can say that I understood my mother's perspective. I just prayed that this never happened between me and Corrine. I loved her, but I definitely could not see her with another dude. Fuck that we better off as friends now, no that was only good for some, my parents were in that category.

"Would you two like desert?" The waitress asked.

Before I could even get a word out to say anything my mother chimed in. "Yes, I am pregnant. I am just his mother though, and I would love a slice of lemon meringue pie." I looked at my mother and shook my head, I couldn't wait to meet my little brother or sister soon.

CORRINE

I had a book signing in Tampa, Florida today that started at 4:00 pm. I was up early because I had to get my hair and nails done before meeting Brenda who was traveling with me. I was getting ready to go to Miami Airport for our hour and nine-minute flight. We were on the plane no later than 2:00pm. For the duration of the ride I sat back and slept, Brenda was reading Eric Jerome Dickey's latest novel with her pink Beats by Dre headphones on her ears. I was excited about this book signing for the women of color who lived in or around the Tampa area. Even though it was geared toward us in the audience you still found women of other races as well, which I also was pleased with knowing that so many loved my work.

"You wanna go to Audrey's for drinks after?" Brenda asks me as I look at her from the window seat of the plane.

"Yeah, I wanna check out the neo-soul music before we come back in the morning." I said.

"Girl, it's pretty decent. The drinks and food just add to the place. When me and Bobby come there to vacation, we always hit up Audrey's." Brenda said referring to her husband of eight years.

"Well, we shall see just how good it is." I added.

The pilot announced that we had just made it to the Tampa Airport and the weather was a good seventy-five degrees with not a cloud in the sky. Brenda and I were staying at the Marriott Suites near the airport for the night. We figured to come back the next day since the book signing did not end until 8:00pm that night. There was going to be a questionnaire session, followed by the mix and mingle which my books would be available for purchasing and autographing. We checked into the hotel at 3:00pm and lucked up on having rooms next to each other.

I called K.J. as soon as I got settled, he told me that he and Kylie were doing okay, and Martha went home for the day, and he ordered Chinese food for dinner. I told him that I would call him tonight, just as soon as the signing was over, and I and Brenda made it back from Audrey's. All of my table supplies were already sent down, along with my books that Centrae Book Store, an African-American owned book store down in Tampa, was here to help in the process of anyone wanting to purchase my books.

The book signing was held at The Tampa Public Library which was huge. The actual signing was in the conference room down stairs. The room seated about eight-hundred people. Once me and Brenda had gotten there, the eight-hundred attendees were all in the room. They applauded me as I made my way through the room and up to the large table that faced them from the stage-like forum that I was on. The emcee announced me to the women, told them how long I had been in the literary industry, the number of books that I have to date right now, family life, and to ask any questions that they had for me.

"Good evening, ladies!" I said to the crowd as they responded back with hellos and good evenings.

"I am excited that you ladies have picked me to be the guest event speaker for The Women of Color of Tampa, Florida, or as you ladies call it W.O.C.O.T.F." I said as they gave me a loud applause. "I am also excited that you ladies have broadened your horizons to celebrate all women of every nationality and color. By allowing other races to participate in this event, this definitely is a way to expand out, not giving up the true meaning but bringing every woman, regardless of their race together for this exciting and awesome event. Now as you know I am Corrine Andersen-Lexington, New York Times bestselling author. If you were to ask me five to six years ago did I think that I was going to land a literary agent, sign to a major New York publishing house, and get the novels that I started writing in college off the ground and into the stores and hands of ladies like you. I would have said, "no". I said as they all laughed. This was my ice-breaker and I was enjoying the fun that I was having.

"I am happy to join the ranks with those that have come before me and I admire reading them when I was in high school. I love the likes of Kimberla Lawson Roby, Eric Jerome Dickey, Omar Tyree, Terry McMillan, even Zane and you ladies know the list goes on-and-on."

One lady in the audience asked me where did I get the dress I had on? And that she loved my Jimmy Choo's. I thanked her and told her my dress was Versace. The topics included being a wife, motherhood, balancing the two, and also what was next and in store for me. I took about thirty minutes on each topic before it was time to move on to the mix and mingle part of the event. I had so much fun taking pictures with the ladies and signing books.

"Where you wanna grab something eat at before we hit Audrey's?" Brenda asked.

"Let's hit that Southern Soul Food place down here. I have a taste for catfish, greens, and some baked macaroni and cheese that I so miss from Kenny's in Chicago." I said to her, as I signed a lady's book, getting ready to take a group picture with three others.

I got up and came around the table to get in the middle facing

the door as the lady taking the picture stood in front of us. I was all

smiles ready for the camera. I looked ahead and notice a strange

man standing in the door dressed in white wearing dark sunglasses.

Something about the way he looked at me with a blank expression

gave me a chill down my back. He noticed I was staring and

brought his head up. I started to shake and tremble, I tried to blink

to maybe make the image go away, but I realized this was not a

dream. I truly was still at the book event and this guy was sitting

way back staring at me.

"Corrine!" A lady said as I screamed and everyone turned their

attention to me.

"Can you please sign my book!" She said giving me a crazy

confused look but smiled.

I came to my senses, embarrassingly smiled at her. I asked her

what her name was, and quickly took out a pen and signed the

inside of her book. She asked for a picture and we took one

together. Her name was Tracey and she had come all the way from

Tallahassee to see me. I thanked her, and she smiled before

walking off. I watched her 'til she got to the other side of the

conference room. Then I quickly turned back towards the main

entrance, my face was stunned, my stomach dropped. I became

uneasy as I looked up for the man but could not see him anymore.

ANGIE

It was around 10:00 pm when I got home for the varsity boys'

basketball game against Carter G. Woodson. So glad that the

weekend was finally here, and that I could unwind and spin

sometime with Mannie who also had been very busy with his

basketball schedule playing for his league. I was already in

preparation for the varsity cheerleaders to get ready for regional

competition. I reflected back to the time when me and Corrine

were doing the same. It sure as hell did not seem like it was

February 2010 already, pushing into March. Add to the win

tonight, which captured the season conference putting the

Centurion varsity boys' basketball team into the playoffs and also

first place.

With myself being overwhelmed by so much going on, the only thing I could think about was my spring break vacation to Corrine and K.J.'s the second week of April. Mannie quickly ran to his room, I yelled for him to shower first before he got into his pajamas and got into the bed which he did. Looking at my cell phone I had three missed calls from my granny right along with a text message that told me to call her no matter what time I got in tonight. I decided to do that once I settled myself, it took me about twenty minutes to do that. I made sure my alarm system was on stay, got in the shower myself and into my pjs with my slippers and house robe. I grabbed a glass of Sutter Home Moscato, turned on Boney James on my stereo system putting it to a low volume just for my ears to hear. I checked on Mannie making sure he was sound asleep, and laid across my sofa in the living room with my candles burning, dialing my grandmother's phone.

"Hello." She said after two rings.

"Granny, you told me to call you." I said.

"Yes! Angie, remember the guy I was telling you about?"

"Yeah." I said taking a sip of the wine.

"Well, I ran into him again tonight and I was like, hot damn. Angie at the game tonight?" I rolled my eyes but continued to listen to her talk about this *oh, so perfect guy* that was just right for me based on her accusations. "So because I know this is fate having it for you, I think you should meet him."

"Say what?" I said turning my face up listening.

"Yes, he's a restaurant owner."

"Okay." I said.

"Okay, my ass! Angie, do you even care because I can stop. You know you are really getting on my last nerve with this attitude like you don't need to get yourself out and date. The way you goin', you gonna be an old ass maid with no man! You really need to stop!" As if I had heard my last of this as well. I sat my glass down on the coffee table, sat up, and began to speak.

"Granny, I really appreciate you going out of your way playing match maker but for the last time, I am okay. You are really putting too much into this. I would really respect it if you just worried about yourself and stop trying to hook me up. I don't need you or mama to find me a man, so you can stop!" I said with an attitude. It was quiet for a few seconds before she spoke again.

"Angie, I am only trying to help. Me and your mother just want you to be happy. You're young and you just wasting time by not living your life."

"But Granny, that's exactly what I am doing, living my life, I got…"

"Go head and say it! Mannie and them cheerleaders! Angie, stop it! You sound like the little old lady that lives in the damn shoe!"

"Well, maybe I want to be that little old damn lady!" I yelled.

"The route you're goin', chile, you already there!"

"Well, just let me be then!" I yelled.

"Fine!" My grandmother yelled.

"Thank you!" I responded back. I could tell that I had struck a nerve with my grandmother. She was very quiet and so was I for the next five minutes before the silence was broken.

"Angie, I just want you to experience some happiness, I am not trying to be mean when I say this but you cannot live your life through Mannie. And you cannot keep lying to yourself that you have moved on from Gino. He's got who he wants to be with, giving her a baby, and I recently saw him on ESPN giving an interview talking about marrying the girl. Angie, you have got to move on! You will love again and find that happiness, but you have got to allow yourself to experience it. Make peace with your past and the future that you will have. All I'm sayin'..."

I hung up on my grandmother. I didn't mean to be disrespectful, but I had heard enough. Reality had kicked in, I did not want to face it, but it finally reared its head. Not only was she pregnant, but he was also going to marry her. The marriage that I would never get, that I knew I deserved. Not to mention Gino had not even told me or Mannie yet. I let out a silent cry, laid my head back on the couch and sobbed myself into a deep sleep.

JEFFERY ROSHELL

K.J.

I chilled at my teammate's, Trevor Brelins, crib after the game

for his big birthday celebration. Trevor had invited all the local

celebrities and the team, even some of the basketball players from

the Miami Heat. A party always brought even the biggest rivals

together for a good time to kick it. Corrine didn't want to come

along after the game, she said that she was tired and just wanted to

go back home, get in the shower, put Kylie to bed once Martha

left, and then get some sleep herself. I told her that I would not be

out to late, and that I would call before I came in. Watching a few

of the highlights from tonight's game on Trevor's big screen TV

they were re-running it, we had killed Seattle 108-91 tonight.

"K.J., bro, them boards don't lie, mane." Trevor said puffing on a Cuban cigar.

"Hell naw!" I replied back watching the game. Trevor had lit up with the board points and assists tonight. Taking a sip of the beer that I had in my hand, I made my way out onto the patio of Trevor's mansion in Fort Lauderdale. The party that he was hosting was really jumping, seems like everybody on the team and from the game was in attendance. I overlooked his back yard where the pool was packed out, and there was a D.J. and a bartender. I even saw a few nice asses in bikinis walking around. Suddenly I felt a female hand touch my back, turning around I damn near dropped the beer bottle off the ledge. Standing in front of me was Shana Fields, the girl who almost stole me from Corrine in high school, not to forget she tried to trap me by getting pregnant, too.

"Kenvarius Lexington." She said smiling. She still looked good even ten years later, she hadn't put on a pound, standing in front of me with a white pantsuit on, her hair in straight back cornrows and a pair of white three-inch-high heels.

183

"Wassup, Shana" I replied. We hugged each other but you could tell it was fake.

"It's funny running into you here at this party? Well, I must have forgotten you play for the Fahrenheit." She said.

"Yep."

"You still look good, man."

"And you do as well." I said.

"Why thank you." She said taking a glass of champagne from the lady that was walking around with a tray of glasses. Shana took a sip.

"What you doing in Miami?" I asked her.

"I came down with my love to have some fun." She said.

I shook my head at her comment. Maybe she had slowed down her ways with her new man, hopefully she left the whorish ways in high school.

"Where's Miss Corrine?" She asked.

"She went home after the game, she was tired." I said shocked hearing her ask about Corrine because they could not stand each other in high school. Corrine had every right, not to mention Corrine was still mad at the day she caught me and Shana at my house and she didn't get to beat her ass like she really wanted to.

"I see that she is writing books, and she's still pretty." Shana said with a smirk taking a sip of her champagne again. I knew that she was being funny when she said Corrine was still pretty.

"Yep, that's my baby." I said smiling glancing at Shana, which I knew kind of got under her skin. She rolled her eyes just a little but sipped the last of her drink looking for a spot to put the glass.

"Well, I am happy for you two. Congrats on the new baby."

"Thanks." I replied. This was truly an awkward moment, I didn't know what else to say at the moment. She looked good and was doing well for herself.

"So how do you like it down here in Miami? Big step up from Chicago ain't it." Shana said.

"You can somewhat say that, I mean I love the hot weather. Would take it over the snow any day, but you know we deal with those hurricanes here." I said.

"That's the only thing about here. I love the weather, too, but being by the gulf with those hurricanes I can deal without. I love living in Vegas." Shana said.

"Oh, so you're in Vegas now?"

"Yep. Been there for the past five years, my mother moved out of the Floyd homes and live in Georgia now. She loves the south and she even stressed that she would not come back to Chicago under any circumstances."

"So are you coming to the class reunion?" I asked her.

"I plan on it. Haven't seen everyone in years even my old crew." She said referring to Kyra, Jasmine, and Vanessa.

In high school they were the popular, loud ghetto hood crew also referred to as the hoes of the school. I remember Kyra tried to have Jasmine and Vanessa jump on Angie at Maude's, the local greasy spoon by the school one early dismissal day our senior year.

Well that plan back fired, Angie's mom ended up showing up pulling out a gun which scared them off. But Angie ended up running up on Kyra in the process and kicking her ass. To this day I am still mad that I was not there to witness that fight. I was at my house with Shana taking advantage of the fact that it was an early dismissal, my mom was at work, and there was no interruption of the sex we were having.

"I would have thought y'all would have still been in touch?" I said her.

"No. You know once you're setting changes in life so does your circle of friends. We all went our separate ways months later after high school graduation." She said.

I understood what she meant by that, even the people I knew from college I ended up losing contact with. Or they will either send me messages to my Facebook page, some of those inboxes I check, others I let my assistant respond to.

"Are you and Corrine looking forward to the reunion?" Shana asked.

"Corrine is definitely lookin' forward to it, it's been all she talks about." I said laughing and so did Shana.

"Well, I'm sure we will run into each other in July. Seems like it's not even that far away."

"Yeah, we got like three, maybe four months. That shit will be here before we blink." I said looking around for Travis who I saw was entertaining a bunch of groupies.

"I'm sure I will see all of you guys there." Shana said.

"Likewise." I replied taking a Cuban cigar out of my shirt pocket, lighting it, and blowing out the smoke.

Shana and I were suddenly greeted by a beautiful chick who was also adorning cornrows to the back of her head, light skin, she had a tattoo on both arms. She looked to be about five feet, eleven inches in height, slim, and she was rocking a pair of Jordan's. She had on a nice all white fit, she looked like Hoops for *Flavor of Love* just a little more masculine. I began to think to myself where I had seen her face from, it came to me that she played basketball in the WNBA for the Los Angeles Team.

"K.J., this is…"

"Sapphire King." I said amazed. She was a damn good b-ball player, a beast on the women's court.

"K.J. Lexington. It's nice to meet you as well." Sapphire said shaking my hand.

I couldn't believe that Shana was friends with Sapphire King. I loved watching her on TV when she played. Her stats were just as good as mine or Kobe Bryant's. I took a pull on my cigar and glanced at Shana and Sapphire. That's when I damn near burned myself watching Sapphire kiss Shana on the lips and pat her ass.

"Bae, I'm goin' to mingle for a second. When you're ready I'll be downstairs by the bar." Sapphire said to Shana.

"I'll be down soon." Shana said as she watched Sapphire walk down the stairs and off towards other party goers, some male and female basketball players, and even Travis walked up to talk to the group that huddled around the bar to order drinks, engaged in deep conversation. I looked at Shana, stunned but it was the thing nowadays, so it didn't so much surprise me that she had went this route now.

"I guess I'll see you at the reunion in July, K.J. It was nice running into you." She said smiling and winking her eye at me as she turned to walk down the winding stair case. I nodded at her, checked the time on the screen on my phone, dabbed the smoke out of the cigar, and decided that it was probably time for me to make it home as well.

MARTHA

It was 9:30 pm once I made it to my condo that was about

fifteen minutes from the Lexington's home. I forgot to turn on my

lights so I could not see anything as I walked in. I locked the door

behind me and laid my purse and keys on my counter top. Before I

could cut the light on in my living room, I heard my entertainment

system come on blasting the last two minutes of Aretha Franklin's

What a Friend We Have in Jesus from her gospel album. I jumped

and screamed when I saw Marcus sitting in my recliner chair

staring at me with a blank expression on his face. He cut the song

off after the last *everything* that the choir and Aretha had loudly

bellowing on the record.

"What do you want?" I asked him.

"You already know what that is, but I just figured it was time to pay you a visit. Haven't seen you in a while." He said in his deep raspy voice that he inherited from his father that sent chills up my back.

"Leave them alone, Marcus. What happened to you was your own fault and you know that!" I said to him as my blood started to boil in my body. I did not like what he was doing and I didn't know how much longer I could hold out on not going to the authorities about what he was doing. The only thing was I did not know where to locate him here in Miami, but he knew my whereabouts all the time.

"I am tired of playin' this game with you. Since you wanna protect her so bad, ain't it bad enough you clean the shit and piss out of her panties and toilet? You protecting her for what? Why?" He asked standing up and looking at me.

"I had no idea she was the one that sent you to prison. And like I said that has nothing to do with the fact that you did what you did. You're out, you need to move on with your life and forget about what happened before you land back there and for good." I said.

Marcus laughed and shook his head at me. "It will be all over soon." He said making a serious face at me.

"And what does that mean?" I asked looking confused.

"You'll see, just keep your eyes and ears open." He said smiling at me which I did not like.

"I just don't know where you went wrong, or how I birthed such a child into this world filled with evil and the devil's ways. This is why I washed my hands of you. I don't want no parts of you and you hurting people! LEAVE THE LEXINGTON'S ALONE!" I yelled at him not liking the remark he made.

"I've just begun what is in store for the Lexington's. "He replied back walking towards my front door.

"You need to leave them be, Marcus. I said leave them alone, and don't ever come by that house again." I said highly upset, my head spinning because God only knows what he had been planning to do to them. To Corrine, I loved her like she was daughter and it would kill me to know that if anything happens to her, K.J., or Kylie, and it was something I could have done to prevent it.

"You're gonna force me to go to the police!" I yelled at him.

Marcus opened the door, stopped and turned, he looked at me and bellowed out, "Well, you better do it soon."

CORRINE

Next week was the first week of April and I could not believe that the time and the new year was going fast. I had started writing my next book and things were coming along rather well with it. I had already gotten to a good twenty thousand words in. My new characters were giving all the right material to write about. I was really excited to hear that again and for the ten-year anniversary of the state championship game played back in 2000, the Thornhill Centurion varsity boys' basketball team took home the state trophy. K.J. called Deon and congratulated him. He also told him that he would be donating a large sum of money to the athletic department for new uniforms for the varsity basketball team and the varsity cheerleaders next year even though they had just got new uniforms this year. I loved how K.J. gave back to our alma mater. It made me so proud that he wanted to see success for a school that was in a low-income middle-class neighborhood.

Angie had informed me that the varsity cheerleaders were state champions, headed to Florida for nationals. She sent me the DVD of the state competition and it was very competitive this year. Thornhill had performed a routine that was very detailed and skilled, never missing a beat, volume was very sharp, and there was no nervousness or rushing of the cheer. Angie had said a silent prayer for them to obtain a high school victory, and once all teams had performed and the announcer was ready to announce who the 2010 IHSA Varsity Cheerleading State Champs, Angie could feel the knots in her stomach. Once the announcer came over the mic and announced who won, Angie said her and the varsity girls hugged each other jumping up and down on the mat. Angie said it was as if her prayers were answered. I certainly was happy for the varsity cheerleaders. They were on their way to Florida for nationals just like we did ten years ago. I told Angie good luck and there's no reason they can't go to Florida and bring a national trophy home. I called my mother once I was tired of typing the novel on my computer. I had not heard from her in a few days, so it would be a good thing to do some much needed catching up with her.

"Hello." She said.

"Ma?" I replied sitting down on my couch on the living room, getting comfortable for our conversation.

"Hey, Corrine, how are things, baby?" She asked.

"They're good. I haven't heard from you in a few days so I figured I would call you to see what you've been up to the last few days."

"Well, nothin' much. Your daddy has been following K.J. and the Fahrenheit, look like they trying to get into the playoffs this season from what he says." My mother said.

"Yeah, they've been doing pretty good this year so far. It is almost that time though." I said smiling thinking about how the spring and summer months were coming in full force soon.

"These days and times are passing, baby. You know time waits on nobody."

"Yes, mama." I said looking at the time on the clock, it was almost 6:00 pm and K.J. was in L.A. playing the Lakers, it was on channel 35. I turned on the TV and saw him take the jump shot and make it as they shouted his name.

"So, what's going on down there next month?"

"Well, Angie is coming here for her spring break, so we're gonna hang out. She's letting Mannie spend that time with Gino." I said.

"That should be nice. I know you haven't seen her since Thanksgiving."

"Yep, so I'm looking forward to it."

"Great, baby, so are you gonna come home before your class reunion or you're pretty much gonna wait until July which is also your birthday month?" My mother asked.

"Yea, the reunion is two weeks after my birthday, so we're gonna wait then to see everyone." I said excited just thinking about it all.

"That's good. So, I talked with Kathryn since Thanksgiving, she is about to be six months pregnant."

"I know. I'm excited for her, K.J. still can't believe it, mama. But I told him that maybe God saw fit for her to have a baby later on in life now." I said.

"Well, it's going to be something. Miss Kylie will have an aunt or uncle younger than her." My mother said which made me laugh a little.

"Yes, quite interesting." I replied noticing that I had a call coming in from Brenda my publicist.

"Mama let me call you back real quick. It's Brenda, my agent."

"Okay, baby. Go ahead just call me back a little later."

"Sure thing, mama." I replied closing that line to answering my other line.

"Hey, Brenda." I said ready to take the call.

ANGIE

Since I hung up on my grandmother three weeks ago, I had not heard from her or my mother. I know my mother was just as upset as my grandmother was for what I had done, but I just could not take the fact that they both were so hard up on finding me a man. Not to mention what my grandmother had let out the bag the day we were on the phone arguing. Gino failed to mention that to me or Mannie that he now had proposed to this girl that he had gotten pregnant. Gino finally called to let me know.

"So when were you going to tell us that you were getting married?" I said not even responding to his hello when I answered. Gino paused before he spoke.

"It was not supposed to come out over the television like that. I wanted to tell you and Mannie first, hell I didn't even tell my own family first."

"But your family already knows who she is. You just up and tell me and Mannie over brunch just a while back that you had a girlfriend, but now a fiancé. Me and Mannie should have known about this the moment you started seeing this woman." I said.

Gino was silent for a while. "I apologize for not discussing this with you first hand, but I knew that you were probably not going to take it well."

"Regardless to how I took it, it is your responsibility to let me and your son know who is in your life now. And please do not go there with me." I said through clenched teeth. He had struck a nerve and now I was definitely ready to go there with him.

"Angela, if you're looking for an apology, here it is. I am sorry for not being what you wanted me to be for this perfect relationship that you thought was going to exist between the both of us. I am sorry for not taking you to college with me to Stanford, and also not marrying you after college. But let's not forget, we both were only eighteen years old when you got pregnant fresh out of high school. I am sorry for just not giving you what you wanted."

"Stop it!" I yelled.

"This is what you wanted to hear all these years, isn't it?" He asked.

"Lose the damn sarcasm!"

"Angie, what do you want from me?"

"I have always wanted you!" I snapped. "Gino, that's all I have ever asked for, is for you to love me the way that I cared about you. Every time we turned around it was something different. Between your on again off again high school girlfriend coming back into the picture the end of our senior year, to our college years being apart at two different schools, even then I would hope that time apart from you would realize how much I meant to you at one point. But it did not work out that way. Here I am, just a basketball player's baby mama." I said as it sadden me how this was so true about the life that had become of us. It took everything in me not to start crying.

"Angie, it really just was not meant for us to be together. Have you ever thought about things seeing it from that perspective?" Gino said.

"No, because I knew that you would eventually come to your senses."

"Senses on what, Angie?" He asked and laughed.

"At times I did, but I did not want to speak that into existence. I just knew that things would turn around, I just knew that you would realize that you had a family right in front of you and you would make things right between the both of us, and we would be together."

"Angie, we were young, too young to know what we know now."

"And that is?" I asked.

"That it just truly was not meant for us."

Here he goes with this shit again. It was so exhausting. How could someone that said they cared for me, tell me that I was not the one for them? I was confused and tired of hearing this, but it was now becoming reality. He just really did not love me like he did when we were in high school.

"Angie, as much as I would have loved to give you that big house, and be the man that you wanted, we were young. I love you, but we were young. I can't explain why I am not the man that you expected me to turn out to be. But the only thing I can say is that things were not meant for us. And I hope you can accept that, as much as we argue. We do have our moments where we can be nice and cordial for Mannie, but I don't love you like I did in high school. And if I have to apologize for that then this is me saying I'm sorry."

I was hearing everything that Gino was saying and like a piercing sharp knife that was going through my heart. I was taking it all in. After all this time, the years that had gone by, this was the moment I dreaded would happen. I did not know if I wanted to break down and cry, or yell some more into the phone. I really loved Gino, and the reality of the situation right now as that he did not love me in the same manner. And was getting ready to start a life with someone else.

"Angie, say something please." Gino said.

"What do you want to hear me say?" I asked after another five second pause.

"I can't speak for you."

"Exactly!" I responded quick. I looked at the clock on the wall, then preceded to talk on the phone.

"I kinda knew that this day was going to come that you were going to be telling me all of this. I pretty much figured it. I didn't want to speak it into existence but here we are. This hurts like hell, I hate the fact that nothing came out of this, but Mannie. I just don't know what to say at this time." I said holding back the tears.

"Angie, you are a great mother. You are a great person. But it was never meant for us to be no more than friends. Mannie drew us more together, but that was it." Gino said.

"I hear you." I say back wiping the tears from my eyes reaching for tissue. There was an awkward silence before he spoke again.

"I have a few errands I have to run soon. I will give you a call next week about the preparations for spring break for Mannie."

"Shit!" I thought out loud. Spring break was coming up in a few weeks, next week was state competition for the varsity cheerleaders. I realized how much I had on my plate. "Okay, and Gino before you go can I say this?"

"Yeah, what's going on?" Gino replied sounding a little puzzled.

"Congratulations on your new baby, your new fiancée, and I hope you have a great new exciting and wonderful life with this lady - whomever she is. But I meant what I said. Mannie is not coming to live with you at all! Now you have yourself a good night, talk to you soon!" I did not wait for a response, but simply hit the end button on my house phone.

CLASS REUNION

K.J.

Corrine was gone out for a book signing some place on South Beach today. It was a lazy day for me with no game until the end of the week or practice 'til tomorrow. So I went and worked out at the gym, and then decided to keep Kylie company while Corrine was out, and Martha worked.

"Mr. Lexington, I sure can't wait for it to get to the summer months again." Martha said as she folded laundry.

"Martha, I love the summers here in Miami. That heat and the parties the celebs and my basketball buddies throw. I love Chicago but my family can keep that cold weather. I'll take this heat and hurricanes any day." I said as she laughed.

"So, Mr. Lexington, was it your high school senior year you said that you almost lost Mrs. Corrine?" Martha asked me.

"Well, I forget that you did want me to finish telling you the story, but yes." I said as Martha quickly grabbed me a beer out of the fridge and I opened it and drank it.

"I'm all ears." She said continuing to fold with a smile.

"Well it's like this, we had broken up because of a girl in our class tried to blackmail me. Corrine swore up and down I had cheated on her with the girl. I actually seen this girl at a party here a few weeks ago and she's dating one of the WNBA players. I guess she prefers the same sex role now. So while I started dating Shana, which is her name, Corrine met this guy named Marcus. I knew something was not right about this dude. Well one night I was at the barbershop he was there, I overheard him having a conversation about making his move on a girl and damn near raping her. When he went into his wallet and showed Corrine's picture I froze up! I was really concerned about her well-being even though we were not together anymore.

"So I had to warn her, at first she did not believe me and thought I was just being jealous of the fact that she had found someone new. But it just so happened the same night that I was at the Floyd home projects in Chicago was the same night he brought her back to his apartment and proceeded to rape her. She got out with nothing but a bruise on her face, I ended up confronting the guy and a big fight broke out. The next thing I knew the police were taking me in handcuffs away, Martha I will never forget it, but I truly believe Corrine has put it all behind her."

"So what happen to the man?" Martha asked all intrigued in my story.

"He's since been in prison. I don't think he's getting out any time soon which is a good thing. Corrine has not seen him since she sent him to prison."

"Wow." Martha responded.

"Yeah, crazy. I'm just glad the guy is locked up and not on the streets. From the history on him, Corrine was not the only one, but she was the lucky one. A few of the other girls came forth when she testified against him in court." I said as me and Martha locked eyes and she looked as if she wanted to cry which was strange. It was as if she knew something, but I quickly blew it off by changing the subject.

"So, my mother is about six months pregnant now with a girl. Kylie will be a one-year old niece, me and Corrine have been thinking about getting her this expensive baby bed from Gucci that we saw online as a gift".

"I'm sure your mother would love it!" Martha said smiling.

"That's why I knew I could ask you, and you would tell me, Martha." I said getting up to put my empty bottle of beer in the trash.

"Mr. Lexington?"

"Yea, Martha." I responded getting ready to go upstairs, Corrine would be back home soon.

"You're a good man and husband to Miss Corrine. You're also a great father to Kylie, almost like the son I wanted."

I looked at Martha, smiled with the response. "Thank you, you're like the second mother we inherited."

"SO, HERE'S WHAT I WANT! I WANT YOU TO GO FORTH WITH THIS PLAN I AM GIVING YOU. IT IS TO BE EXECUTED IN THIS FORM. I WANT YOU TO KILL CORRINE, BREAK THAT NIGGA OF HER'S KNEE CAPS SO HE DON'T PLAY BALL NO MORE, AND STAB THAT DAMN BABY TO DEATH. AND IF THERE IS ANYONE ELSE IN THAT DAMN HOUSE YOU KILL THEM TOO! THOSE ARE SPECIFIC ORDERS."

LOOKING OVER TO THE SIDE WAS A TALL SIX-FOOT-FOUR DARK COMPLEXED DRED-HEAD HAITIAN TAKING ORDERS FROM MARCUS. THE HAITIAN WENT BY THE NAME OF KEET, HE WAS A KNOWN HIT MAN THROUGHOUT THE SOUTHERN MIAMI/HAITI BORDER.

SUCCESSFULLY CARRYING OUT ALL HIS PLANS OF ACTION, LEAVING NO STONES UNTURNED, AND NO TRACES OF EVIDENCE TOWARD HIS PATH. HE WAS HIGHLY RECOMMENDED TO MARCUS FROM AN ACQUAINTANCE DOWN NEAR THE HAITIAN BORDER TO MIAMI.

"WHEN ARE YOU TRYING TO GET THIS DONE?" KEET ASKED LIGHTING A ROLLED JOINT INHALING THE SMOKE THEN BLOWING IT OUT INTO THE AIR.

"FEW WEEKS FROM NOW! I WAS GOING TO WAIT UNTIL THE BITCHES HIGH SCHOOL CLASS REUNION, BUT I FIGURE I KNOCK HER AND HER FAMILY OFF NOW. IT WILL BE FINALLY DONE".

"FEW WEEKS AIN'T TELLIN' ME SHIT MAN, I'M BOOKED. AT ANY MINUTE AT ANY TIME AND…"

MARCUS SLAMMED A HEAVY BAG ON A TABLE FILLED WITH EIGHTEEN ROLLED STACKS OF ONE HUNDRED DOLLAR BILLS. 'KEET PICKED UP THE BAG

FILLED WITH THE MONEY, HE LOOKED AT MARCUS

LIKE HE HAD SEEN A GHOST AND REPLIED.

"WHO IS THIS BITCH AGAIN?"

CORRINE

"Angie, I cannot wait for you to get here in three weeks! K.J. will be in Atlanta for three days, that will give us enough sister time." I said excited as ever on my Blackberry.

"I knowwww! Can you believe that the varsity cheerleaders made it back to nationals, I can feel it Corrine. This just might be Thornhill's year."

"Yes! I am so happy for them. They're a really good team just like our varsity ten years ago."

"Well, we shall see. I'm just excited that we are finally going back to nationals after all these years." Angie said. I really didn't want to break the ice on the subject but I knew that Angie was looking for me to say something about it ever since she told me a few weeks ago.

"So have you talked to Gino since?" I asked her.

"Girl, no. After I said what I meant again with Mannie he basically has just been calling to talk to him and that's it. Or if he wants to know if Mannie needs anything his ass will just text me and that's it. Girl, I don't even care no more. I was really hurt, but fuck him, fuck love, fuck it all!"

"Angie, girl, you will find someone. Right now just keep your focus on what's important, the fact that you are doing the damn thing, girl. When you least expect it, love will find you." I said reassuring her of something that she already knew.

With our sisterhood bond over all these years we were able to encourage each other when we were going through our ups and downs. That's what good friends were for, and me and Angie were more like sisters than best friends.

"Corrine, it's 2010! I am single and look good for twenty-eight years of age. I guess you can say I've been thinking about it, and I am so ready for this class reunion in July."

"Yayyyy!" I screamed into the phone and Angie laughed.

"Yes, you can say that you changed my mind on things. I'm gonna go and have some fun and see what them people we went to school with have been up too!"

"Girl, let me tell you who K.J. saw at one of his teammates parties a minute back." I said not trying to cut Angie off, but I knew there was something I had to tell her.

"Who?" She asked just as excited knowing that it was going to be good whatever I had to tell her.

"Shana Fields, girl! Shana Fields!"

"What?!" Angie yelled.

"Yes. And you will not believe who she is dating now which really shocked the hell out of me." I said.

"Corrine, is she dating a basketball player?"

"Yep, but not just anybody." I said.

"And what do you mean by that?" Angie asked.

"Let's just say she's playin' for the other team."

"Get the fuck out of here! She's a Lesbian now???" Angie shouted.

"Girl, I could not believe it when K.J. told me. He says she's dating some girl from the WNBA."

"Uhhmm..." Angie replied.

"I wonder what the rest of her crew is doing?" That was a good question.

I wondered what the other girls that she hung with in high school were doing as well. Kyra, Jasmine, and Vanessa I remember when they tried to jump Angie senior year of high school, and that plan backfired on them. Kyra and Angie ended up fighting and Angie won, to this day Angie still mentions that fight from time to time.

"Well, we will see at this class reunion now won't we." Angie said.

"I'm off to bed soon. I have a radio engagement in the morning." I said feeling myself get tired.

"Alright, well I will talk to you later."

"Later." I replied to Angie.

"Bye." Angie said hanging up the line.

ANGIE

Here it was the end of March, next week I would be traveling

to Florida for the national high school cheerleading competition in

Orlando with the Thornhill varsity cheerleaders. Then two weeks

after that I would be in Miami with Corrine. Time could not speed

itself up any faster. Then adding to that Thornhill's varsity boys'

basketball team took home the state trophy and was the 2010

champs. Things were going pretty good in life right now if I did

say so myself.

My grandmother needed me to come along with her to some

sort of new Soul Food Restaurant that opened near downtown

Chicago. I had heard about it and figured let me try it since

Shavela and everyone else raved so much about it. Bee Bee's was the name, and they had just opened a third location up north near Edgewater.

"Granny, I sure do hope this food is good like everyone talks about." I said as me and her cruised on Lake Shore Drive, while she sat on the passenger side.

"Baby, I assure you the food is delicious. Me and your mother ate here about a week or so ago and I said that I just had to bring you up here to taste it for yourself."

"Okay, I'll take your word for it." I said.

My grandmother smiled at my comment as we pulled into Bee Bee's Soul Cuisine. We admired how fancy and stylish it looked on the outside, my grandmother telling me just how the building accentuated elegance and beauty for it to be a soul food restaurant. I had to admit, she was right. There was a nice crowd here for a Wednesday night, I found a parking spot in the back of the restaurant, and we both got out and walked to the front doors.

"Chile, I will be glad when it gets warm here in Chicago." My grandmother said throwing her long shawl over her. She hated the winters but loved here for the Chicago summers.

"Who you telling?" I agreed turning my attention towards the hostess who walked up to greet us.

"Welcome To BeeBee's. How many?" She politely asked.

"Just two." I responded.

"Can we get a booth, please?" My grandmother said.

"Sure thing, ma'am. Not a problem follow me." The hostess said as we walked behind her.

I loved their uniforms a nice dark, blue polo shirt that said Bee Bee's with khaki pants, and they were allowed to wear gym shoes which was a good thing working a job where you were on your feet most of the day. The hostess sat me and my grandmother down at a nice booth for two in the middle part of the restaurant.

"I hope you ladies enjoy, my name is Ariana. And your waitress, Aileen will be here shortly." She said as we thanked her, and she went back to the front of the restaurant.

"I liked her braids." My grandmother said as we both thanked Ariana and she walked back towards the front.

"They were nice. I think I'm going to tell mama to do some of those for me before I go to Corrine's." I said.

"When you leaving again?" My granny asked.

"In about two weeks."

"I know you excited."

"Granny, I am so ready for this vacation. Especially coming back from nationals with the cheerleaders after next week." I said.

"I remember when you and Corrine, and the varsity squad your senior year went to Florida for nationals. I know they probably go the same momentum."

"Excited ain't the word. I just can't believe it all, ten years later." I said as a short brown-skinned girl came up and I knew it had to be Aileen, our waitress.

"Hello, I'm Aileen, your waitress for this evening. Can I start you off with anything to drink? Appetizers?"

"Can I get a water with lemon." My granny said.

"And you ma'am?" She asked me.

"Coke is fine." I said.

"Coming right up." She said walking away. I looked at the menu and everything looked delicious. I did not know what I wanted more as an entrée and sides. The smothered or fried chicken, greens, mac and cheese, then they had pork chops, lamb chops, baked chicken, meatloaf, one thing I knew, I was hungry. I talked with my grandmother about other things that I had coming up since the summer was approaching. Mannie would be getting ready for the fourth grade, and I would be knocking on twenty-nine's door. My Grandmother made a face at something she ate and quickly called Aileen over.

"Honey, is there a bit of hot pepper in my greens you brought me?" She asked still slightly coughing as well.

"Why yes, ma'am, did you not want pepper in the greens?"

"Honey, no I can't take hot pepper in my greens like this."

"Not a problem, ma'am. I am so sorry and will take it back." Aileen said taking the plate from my grandmother and rushing to the back.

Now this was all new to me, I had no idea my grandmother could not take hot spice in her greens, this had to be something new. I asked her was there anything wrong with the smothered pork chops and mac and cheese she had, she said no. I ordered the blackened catfish and spring rice.

"Granny, you okay?" I asked her.

"Yeah." She said as she coughed but turned her attention toward a guy that walked over to the table. I'm assuming to talk to her about the food. I looked up but could not take my eyes off him, he was about 5'11 dark brown-skinned. I could tell he worked out, and he was wearing that Paris Hilton for men fragrance dressed down in a polo khaki pants and Stacey Adam dress shoes. His teeth even glistened white as he laughed and talked with my grandmother. He almost looked like a fine ass football player dressed up after the game, you know when they do their press conferences and all, but I could not take my eyes off of him. It was as if I knew him from somewhere but could not pin-point it yet.

"Miss Tralonda, how are you this evening?"

"Dee, I'm fine. I had to find out if you were here tonight?" The Dee guy smiled at my grandmother, then he looked at me.

I went from curious to puzzled. I was confused on what the hell was going on, and I knew my grandmother was full of shit with that no spice in her greens story. That's all she put in her greens whenever she made them.

"Okay, what's going on granny?" I asked her still looking at the Dee guy who stared at me and for some reason it was as if he knew me, but I could not think about from where?

"Hello, Angie." He said.

Don't Ask My Neighbor By The Emotions came on over the sound system. I still looked puzzled and shook my head back and forth wondering who he was.

"Damn, Dee. Boy, tell this girl who you are!" My grandmother said with excitement.

The mystery guy looked at me for a second. Then he spoke in his deep voice as the hair stood up on the back of my neck and I damn near pushed my glass of Coke off the table onto the floor.

"Angie, it's David. David Baine from high school."

It made perfect since, Bee Bee's, David's parents were always wealthy. I was in total shock because he looked nothing like he did in high school. We even dated for a while and right now I was also feeling guilty for the way that I treated him because of my own foolish young dumb ways, he probably was married with kids.

"Angie, I told you I had someone for you to meet. Well, this is him. I've been coming here quite often and me and David held a conversation discovering that he was your old high school boyfriend. So I thought why not bring you up here for good food and to surprise you with seeing him." She said.

"Granny, David, I am really lost for words. I have not seen David since we graduated high school." I said looking at him with a half-smile.

Part of me was shocked and the other part was still a little guilty. David had changed, and he was definitely looking damn good now.

"Well, I'm sure you and David got some catching up to do? It's been ten years." My grandmother said looking at us both.

Aileen brought her food out in a to-go container with it inside a BeeBee's bag. I looked toward the door and saw Ernie, the deacon for Powerhouse that my grandmother was dating coming through the door.

"Hey, baby. Thanks for coming to get me and take me home. Angie is here catching up with an old friend and I did not want to be a third wheel." My grandmother said as she rose up, gathered her bag, and she started going in her purse for her debit card to pay for the meal. But I told her I had it, and then David chimed in and said no it was on him.

"I owe you a cooked meal. Thank you, baby." My granny said to David with a smile as her and Ernie walked towards the front. Ernie said goodnight to both me and David, my grandmother said that she would call me later.

"It's really been ten years, Angie?" David asked breaking the silence that was there for a quick second.

"I still cannot believe it is you? Oh my, God you look so different, David." I said.

He smiled and said, "Yea, and you still look good, too." I smiled and dropped my head a little. "Did you want something else to drink?" He asked me.

"No. I don't need nothing else to drink. I have to drive all the way back to the south suburbs when I leave here." I said.

"Oh, where are you now living if you don't mind me asking?"

"In Frankfort." I said to him.

"Would you at least like water?"

"Yes, David, I'll take a water and lemon." I said as he insisted on getting me something to drink. Aileen brought out the glass of water filled with ice and a lemon wedge on the side with a straw. I took a sip, Mikki Howard's *Baby Be Mine* started playing and I waved my hand in the air a little like I was at church. David laughed at me.

"Y'all jammin' old school up in here. This is really nice, David. I would have never guessed you owned Bee Bee's."

"Yep, my parents are about to add a third location."

"Third? Where is the other one besides this one?" I asked him.

"It's in Boilingbrook. We were trying for Parkersville. On the land where Maude's use to be but somebody had already purchased that property. However, our third location is going up in Milwaukee." He said turning his attention quickly towards one of the other hostesses that needed his signature on something that he gave and return his attention back to me.

"So your parents run all the restaurants?"

"No. They run the one in Bolingbrook which is our main location that's been open for five years now. I run this location here in Edgewater, and my uncle will run the Milwaukee location."

I could not believe how good David and his family had done for themselves since we were in high school. I had heard about the Bee Bee's Soul Food Restaurants, but never would have thought it would have been David from high school and his family that owned them.

"I enjoyed the food." I said to him.

"I'm glad you did." He replied.

"So how has life treated you?" He asked me.

"It has been a journey these past ten years. I have a son with NBA Basketball player Gino Aiello. I'm the head varsity cheerleading coach at Thornhill and a math teacher there also. Not married, single, not dating, it's just me and my son, Emanuel." I said.

"Oh yeah, I remember that you guys were seeing each other. The reason you passed out on stage at graduation was because you were pregnant. I really thought that you guys would have been married with more kids." David said looking at me.

"Yeah. Well he's getting married soon and also expecting another child." I said sipping my water again. David changed gears.

"Well, as for me I have my B.S. in Business Management. Going for my Masters now at DePaul University. I was seeing someone but she felt that her life right now was in another state, and not to be tied down in a relationship in Illinois, so she left. I've been single for two years now. No kids, not dating anyone either." David said.

Damn, I said to myself. I was crazy as hell, she was crazy for letting this man get away. David always had a good heart, that's what I admired the most about him.

"Well, it seems life has dealt us some really crazy hands these past years."

"Crazy is too simple to call it." He said and we both laughed.

"When I found out your grandmother was who she was I had her set this up to bring you up here. Especially since she just kept saying you were still single." David said.

I made a face and told him about the argument that I had with her about dating. "Well I'm glad that I came with her tonight." I said smiling. I had not smiled like this in a while.

"David, I just want to apologize for the way I treated you in high school. My attitude was completely shitty, and I was young. I know it might not mean anything, but I am sorry." I said still feeling some sort of guilt.

"Angie, it's okay. That was ten years ago, we're grown adults now." I felt like a burden had been lifted off my chest accepting his forgiveness. We talked for two more hours, then I had to end my night and get home. We exchanged numbers, and I talked to David until I got home, then called my grandmother and talked to her about the date and went to sleep. All she really wanted to know was after all that, would I be seeing David again? I told her that we had a date for the weekend coming up, she told me if I needed anyone to watch Mannie she would.

235

CLASS REUNION

I WALKED IN MY MOTHER'S HOUSE ON HER, NOT GIVING ONE FUCK, OPENING THE DOOR AND SLAMMING IT.

"YOU MUST HAVE LOST YOUR DAMN MIND, MARCUS! COMING IN MY DOOR AT FOUR AM IN THE MORNING! WHAT THE HELL IS WRONG WITH YOU?" SHE YELLED SITTING UP AND CUTTING HER LIGHT ON.

"NOTHIN', BUT IT'S GETTING' READY TO GO DOWN I JUST THOUGHT I WOULD COME BY AND LET YOU KNOW." I SAID BREATHING HARD AS MY ADRENALINE RUSHED, AND MY NERVES WERE DOING THINGS ALL OVER.

"WHAT'S GETTING READY TO GO DOWN? I TOLD YOU LEAVE THE LEXINGTON'S ALONE".

"NO!" I YELLED.

"LEAVE THEM PEOPLE BE!!!" MY MOTHER YELLED BACK.

"I JUST CAME TO WARN YOU. I KNOW YOU WORK THERE BUT YOU NEED TO BE GONE BY 7PM EVERYDAY WITHIN THE NEXT TWO WEEKS."

"AND WHY IS THAT?" SHE SAID LOOKING AT ME LIKE I LOST MY DAMN MIND.

"I TOLD YOU. I'M GONNA KILL THAT BITCH AND HER FAMILY AND YOU DON'T NEED TO BE THERE. SO I'M GIVING YOU A HEADS UP WARNING. GET OUT BEFORE 7PM EVERY DAY WITHIN THE NEXT TWO WEEKS."

"I'M NOT DOING A THING." SHE SAID LOOKING AT ME.

"FINE, MAMA! I'M DONE!" I SAID WALKING

TOWARDS THE DOOR. SHE CALLED OUT MY NAME, BUT

I HAD QUICKLY SLAMMED HER DOOR, LOCKING IT

BEHIND ME.

K.J.

I packed my last bag for L.A. I would be down there for a week and a half. Corrine was expecting Angie in about an hour, which would give them some much needed girls time. Deon was meeting me in L.A. so that would give us some time to chop up things. I was really proud of that dude for coaching the varsity team at Thornhill and bringing home another state championship trophy. I talked to my mom and she updated me about her pregnancy.

"Baby, have fun in L.A. and bring me back something nice." Corrine said smiling at me.

"What would you like?"

"Surprise me." She said getting up and picking Kylie up out of her walker to feed her a bottle before she laid her down for a light nap. It was 5 pm here in Miami. Martha came down the steps with her bags almost as if she was in a hurry. I noticed lately, that she had been acting very strangely which I brought up to Corrine. She was always in a hurry and she seemed like she had something on her mind. I could not pin-point what it was, but she definitely was troubled about something.

"Martha, you okay?" I asked startling her a little.

"Uhm, yes, Mr. Lexington. I am fine. Just getting my things together I have a few relatives in town. I'm excited and nervous about seeing them, very good people. Just haven't seen them in years." She said giving me a half smile looking at me.

"How long are they in town?" I asked her.

"Just for a few days, but I don't want to miss them because they have my address, but not my phone number to call me." I looked at Corrine, she looked at me like okay, and something was not right with Martha and I could tell it.

"Well, if you need help with making sure you get to them before they depart, I can have Doug, my driver, make sure that you get to them in enough time." I offered.

"No, that's okay." She replied rushing back up the stairs to get her purse and jacket. It was seventy degrees on this April night."

"Corrine, something is going on with Martha." I whispered as loud as I could.

"K.J., I told you nothing is going on with her. She's excited about seeing her family whom she has not seen in years. Bae, believe you me, if something else was going on she would have told me."

"I don't know, I'm not convinced." I said getting up to get me something to drink. My flight was leaving in a few hours and I wanted to make sure that Martha got to her destination before I got on the plane and left. Her attitude and behavior was making me nervous.

"Okay, Mr. and Mrs. Lexington, I am gone for the evening. Mr. Lexington have a safe trip to and back. Mrs. Lexington I will see you Monday morning, early."

"Okay." Me and Corrine said in unison.

"Hey, Martha. You sure you don't want me to make sure that you get home okay?" I asked her again.

"Oh no, Mr. Lexington I'm fine. Just wanna catch my relatives before they go back to Haiti." She said still nervous but trying to remain calm.

"Well, let us know that you're home safe." I said.

"I will." She responded walking out the door to her car.

"Baby, I don't know I still think something is up with Martha."

"Like what, K.J.?" Corrine asked as she cut the TV down and turned her attention toward me.

"I can't think of it, but something does not seem right with her. She is definitely acting really strange, she's been like that the last few days."

"I say it's her relatives, she's just excited to see them, baby. Nothing is going on." Corrine said giving me a bear hug around the waist since she was so much shorter than me.

"Well, if I need to come home early let me know." I said.

"No, sir, you have fun in L.A. Enjoy your time with Deon, cause me and Angie about to relax and have fun. I wish Shavela could have come but we will see her a few months at the class reunion."

"Yep." I said kissing Corrine on the lips. I picked Kylie up and kissed her on her right cheek and laid her back down in the bassinette.

"Doug, should be here in a minute. When is Angie supposed to get here?" I asked Corrine.

"She said that she would call me as soon as she got off the plane and was in route. But you're not going to miss her because she will be here before you leave." Corrine said.

"That's cool." I said.

Corrine's phone started ringing. "That's her." She said answering it.

Corrine screamed which let me know that Angie had arrived and would probably be pulling up at any minute now. I shook my head, laughed a little, and called my dad to let him know about my L.A. trip. Not even ten minutes into the conversation I heard the doorbell ring and Corrine yelled "That's her!!!" Angie came through the door and Corrine hugged her like they were long lost sisters reuniting after years of being separated.

"K.J.!" She said giving me a hug.

"What's up. How was your flight?" I asked her.

"Okay, besides the fact that a couple with a whining ass babies sat they're asses right behind me. I must have looked at the mother, like damn, about a thousand times." She said. We all laughed. Doug had brought in Angie's bags from the car, taking mine out and putting them in the car.

"How long you gonna be gone?" Angie asked me.

"Just a few days. Deon meeting me down there. Clevon was supposed to come but I heard him and Shavela couldn't get a babysitter for them for spring break?"

"Yep, ain't nobody messing with they're kids. Shit, my mother has Mannie because Gino has an away game out of L.A." Angie said.

Realizing the time I kissed Corrine on the lips again. I told Angie see her later, too, and met Doug outside getting into the truck to be transported to the airport.

I WATCH THE TRUCK WITH THAT NIGGA LEAVE THE PREMISES OF THE HOUSE. NOT SURE WHO THE CHICK WAS THAT GOT OUT AT FIRST AND WENT INTO THE HOUSE, BUT I DID SEE BAGS SO I KNEW THE BITCH WAS THERE TO STAY FOR A FEW DAYS. I PICKED UP MY CELLPHONE TO DIAL MY MOTHER.

"I'M OUTSIDE THE HOUSE."

"I'VE BEEN LOOKING FOR YOU. DON'T YOU DO NOTHIN' AND I MEAN IT!" MY MOTHER SAID.

"I TOLD YOU WHEN I STRIKE YOUR GOING TO LEAST EXPECT. I SEE THERE IS NEW COMPANY AT THE HOUSE.

WELL SHE SHOULD HAVE NEVER CAME. I'M TAKING
EVERYONE OUT THAT IS THERE." I SAID.

"LIKE I SAID DON'T YOU DO NOTHIN' STUPID,
MARCUS! AND I MEAN IT!"

"MAMA, IF YOU HAVE NOTHIN' ELSE TO SAY I HAVE
ONE MORE PHONE CALL." I SAID TIRED OF HEARING
THE SAME SHIT.

"YOU HEARD WHAT I SAID!"

"NO, YOU HEARD WHAT I SAID! NOW I'M TIRED OF
TALKIN'. THAT BITCH AND ANYBODY ELSE IN THE WAY
IS ABOUT TO BE GONE. YOU JUST MAKE SURE YOU'RE
NOT IN HARMS WAY AT THE TIME."

"I'M GOIN' TO THE POLICE!" MY MOTHER SAID
HANGING UP THE LINE.

"YOU SHOULD HAVE BEEN WENT." I SAID
SARCASTICALLY WALKING BACK TO MY TRUCK. I
MADE A QUICK PHONE CALL TO KEET TO LET HIM

KNOW THAT WE HAD A NEW PERSON AT THE HOUSE

THAT WOULD NEED TO BE KNOCKED OFF AS WELL.

ANGIE

It didn't even seem like I had been in Miami for three days already, but I was loving the trip and stay. No students, cheerleaders, and my much-needed break from my beloved man child, Mannie. I was loving it. Oh, speaking of the cheerleaders, well we went to Florida nationals and it was as if God was there. We took home the 2010 national high school trophy home. They had told me in the process of them announcing Thornhill had won I passed out and they had to call the paramedics. This was a dream come true, Egypt and the girls worked hard, they were the best varsity cheerleading squad in the state of Illinois, as well as the world. And they proved just that in Orlando.

When I would return, I would be throwing a big celebration for them, invited both the junior varsity and freshman cheerleaders as well. I could not believe it, we had gotten so much media publicity from the local news stations, not to forget that the varsity basketball boys' team had won State this year. Thornhill had made noise getting ready to close out this year.

"Good morning!" Corrine said to me as she walked down the stairs from her room.

"Girl, you can tell that I am getting old as hell. I can't kick it like we used to when were in college." I said bugging my eyes out which made Corrine laugh.

"Yes, we are pushing thirty." Corrine said going into the kitchen. She had on a robe and a bonnet on her head which made me laugh when I noticed it.

"What's funny?" She asked looking at me crazy.

"Your head and that robe, lookin' like my grandmamma." I said continuing to laugh as she told me to shut the hell up. I jumped up and started dancing to The Emotions *I Don't Wanna Loose Your Love* as the old school video came on B.E.T.

"Remember we used to dance to this when your mama threw them barbeques in the summer and I was invited?" Angie said as we started to do the bump.

"Girl, yes. And my uncles and aunts use to do the soul train line and then we would get up and mock them." She said stopping to go get Kylie 'cause we heard her crying upstairs.

"Be right back." Corrine said as the video ended and I turned the music down.

I saw that I had a text from David saying, *Good Morning.* I responded back with, *Good Morning to you Mr. Baine*, adding an emoji smiley face to it. Since the first initial date, I really had been enjoying David's company. To think that my attitude was like it was in high school I really felt a sense of guilt, but it was as if my prayers were answered and I had someone to go out with. And I was grateful to have someone to have a good time with, plus Mannie liked him.

Corrine came back ten minutes later with Kylie, she was dressed in her little outfit. I could tell Corrine gave her a bath in the baby tub 'cause she looked refreshed and her curly head was brushed. I took her from Corrine and started lightly patting her back as I held her and sang to her and she cooed in my ear. I missed the smell and feel of a baby, I wanted one more but that was going to be it.

"So, my line sister's niece is going to keep Kylie tonight. So we can hit South Beach." Corrine said.

"Cool, where we going?" I asked sitting down on the couch with Kylie.

"We can either do McGiver Shores or Bestrows, I mean they both jump but I would prefer Bestrows because McGiver Shores is more for the singles. The people who tend to creep, and that's all that I would need would be for paparazzi to report and send pictures that NBA Star K.J. Lexington's wife is out and about in the Miami night life acting like she is not a married woman with a child." Corrine said shaking her head.

"Girl, fuck them." I said. *A Different World* came on with Aretha Franklin singing the opening hook.

"As much as I definitely can and want to say that, you know how that goes." Corrine said getting out pots and pans to make breakfast.

"It's easy. *Fuck you, middle finger to the camera!*" Angie said and demonstrating as I laughed. Corrine shook her head and asked me did I want bacon or sausage? I told her both and she split the meats up.

"Two months until the class reunion." I said.

"Girl, I am so ready. You should see the dress I got that I am going to make sure I keep my workouts up with my trainer, so I can get into it. I'm ready to see how everybody looks now." Corrine said dropping the meat down into the skillet to fry.

"Fat, ugly, fat, ugly and did I just mention fat, and fuckin' UGLYYY!" I yelled.

"You know Kyra is First Lady Kyra Treybolt?" Corrine said looking at me.

"Oh yeah? I heard her ass done got saved now." I said rolling my eyes.

"Yeah it's not too far from Powerhouse. Her and Pastor Treybolt's church. I just could not believe it, Kyra Simpson a first lady. There definitely is a God." Corrine said and we both laughed.

"Yea, well let's see how she reacts when she finds out her home girl is a lesbian." I said and Corrine made a face saying ain't that a mess.

"Girl, love who you love, but Shana that tried to take K.J. from you. Girl, tried to trap him by trying to save his sperm in a condom to get pregnant she will always be a "dirty bitch" in my book." I said.

"A *dirty bitch* with a girlfriend!" Corrine added.

"Corrine, you messy." I said laughing.

"Whatever!" She said taking cooked meat out of the skillet and placing it on the plate. She started doing the eggs and the toast which I put Kylie in her walker to help her out with.

"Call Shavela." I said to her.

"Okay." She said dialing her number on the house phone and putting her on speaker.

"What you doin'?" I asked when she picked up.

"Girl, just got the hell up. What the hell you hoes doin'?" She asked sounding like her breath still stank.

"Up making breakfast. Get up, shit." I said laughing.

"Girl, I'm going back to bed it's way too early." Shavela said.

"Alright, well gone on back to sleep." I said to her.

"I was gonna do that regardless if you was getting off the line with me or not. You bitches call me later." She said as I called her a bitch too and she laughed before she hung up.

Once breakfast was fixed, we ate and talked. I made mimosas for us. Corrine decided to get dress, told me to do the same so that we could go and site-see in Miami and Ft. Lauderdale. I went upstairs to the guest room that had a bathroom in it where I was staying. My phone started ringing, I looked at the screen it saw that it was David on it.

"Did I catch you at a bad time?" He asked.

"No. I was just about to jump in the shower though. How are you?" I asked him.

"Doin' good. How's the weather in Miami?" He asked.

"It is eighty-five degrees already, and not a cloud in the sky." I said smiling getting out a sun dress, my underwear, and a pair of all white ladies low top Chuck Taylors.

"Man, it is only fifty-four degrees here back home with rain." David said.

"Why does that not surprise me for Chicago. You know I have thought about relocating later on in life." I said.

"Well, hopefully you can take me with. We have a restaurant planted wherever the move is." David replied, and I laughed. I was enjoying this new laughter, this new me, it had only been a few weeks but this new feeling that David was giving me, I just wanted it to become more and more each day.

"Well, let me get in the shower. Me and Corrine have a few places to hit today, and we plan on going out tonight for drinks."

"Alright, hit me later. Enjoy the day, beautiful." David said.

"And you do the same, my love." I replied smiling on the out and as well as inside.

K.J.

"Bro, how long on them wings and fries? My ass is hungry than a bitch!" Deon said looking around for the waitress.

We had decided on Hooters in L.A. for the night, the game against The Seventy-Sevens we won 102-98 and the Nike photoshoot was another success. I did a group pose with a few other athletes and it was going on the cover of Sports Illustrated next month.

"So how about them boys from Thornhill." I said proud drinking my beer.

"Bro, I knew them boys was gonna show out! We had a definite good season, bro."

"Well, I have took the liberty of writing a check for new uniforms for the team as well as the cheerleaders." I said.

"Bro, we appreciate it! You and Nike and the uniforms, we done had so many that West-South is jealous and started trying to keep up." Deon said as the waitress sat his Buffalo wings and fries down in front of him.

"Stanley is killing it overseas." I said digging into the snow crab that was sat down in front of me.
"Saw some of them tapes. That boy is a beast over there in Hungary." Deon said asking the waitress for another beer.

"I spoke with him after the Thornhill - West-South game during Thanksgiving, he was telling me how he loves it better than being in the NBA at times, the perks and all."

"Hell, yeah, K.J. Perks be a mofo, bro, and the money."

"Man, I almost packed Corrine up and told her we were going overseas. Money is top dollar over there." I said as I saw two chicks approaching our table.

"Hey, K.J., can we get a picture with you?" They both asked as I stood up and got in the middle and they both got on one side of me as Deon took the picture.

"Thanks so much" they both said giving me a hug.

"'Preciate the love." I said back as they walked away smiling.

"Bro, that has got to be crazy. Every time you are out and to get that type of attention?" Deon asked.

"Use to it now - me and Corrine. If somebody not noticing me, they notice her because of the books." I said.

"Man, I could only wish one day, bro. I really am happy for you. You got the career, fine ass wife, beautiful daughter, living in Miami with a bad ass crib, and another bad ass crib in Chicago. Man, one day for me, boy, is all I can say." Deon said.

"Bro, I wish you nothin' but success as well, and just be patient, Judy just might be the one. Hell, don't rush it. We ain't even thirty yet." I said ordering another beer.

"Yea, you're right. Ain't tryin' to end up like Clevon."

"Bro! Man, that's a whole 'nother conversation." I said laughing and so did he.

"To think that him and Shavela would have got together. They didn't even like at each other in high school, not sure how that one happened?"

"If I had an explanation for it, bro, I would be able to narrow it down. But I cannot and don't have an answer to that one." I said eating more snow crab and Deon laughed.

"Well, I told that dude, y'all have a good love/hate relationship. They cuss each other out but they back to loving each other in five minutes. Man, is that what love is about, bro?" I said laughing.

"I guess, but I don't want it." Deon said.

"Man." I said thinking if things were like that for me and Corrine, I don't know how we would withstand or last. Just counting my blessings, bro." I said holding up my beer bottle.

"Counting mine, too!" Deon said as we clicked our beer bottles and each took swigs.

JEFFERY ROSHELL

LAYING LOW FOR THE RIGHT AMOUNT OF TIME, MARCUS KNEW THAT IT WAS TIME. HE SPOKE WITH 'KEET AND TOMORROW NIGHT WAS GOING TO BE JUST THE RIGHT TIME TO EXECUTE THE PLAN AND PUT IT INTO ORDER. THINGS HAD CHANGED JUST A LITTLE. WITH HIS MOTHER OFF WORK HE DID NOT HAVE TO WORRY ABOUT HER BEING IN THE MIDST OF THINGS. A SMILE CREPT ON HIS FACE, CORRINE WOULD GET WHAT SHE DESERVED HE THOUGHT! HE HAD WAITED FOR THIS MOMENT FOR DAYS, WEEKS, AND MONTHS.

"SO WHAT TIME DO YOU WANT ME OVER THERE?" KEET ASKED.

"8:30PM, LEAVE NO STONE UNTURNED, ANYONE THERE KILL THEM - PERIOD! I WANT EVERYONE THERE DEAD. IT'S JUST TOO DAMN BAD THAT DUDE OF HER'S AIN'T BACK YET. I WOULD JUST WANT HIS KNEE CAPS BROKEN, KILLING HER AND THAT DAMN BABY WITH TWO BROKEN KNEES WILL DO HIM IN FOR THE REST OF HIS LIFE."

"AI'IGHT, I GOT DIRECTION, AND LOCATION. JUST READY TO GO IN AND DO THIS SHIT TOMORROW NIGHT".

"TOMORROW NIGHT!" MARCUS SAID AND ENDED THE CALL.

CORRINE

It was just too unreal that it was time for Angie to go back home today, we really had bonded like old times these past couple of days. I was on the phone with Brenda discussing an upcoming book signing event. Angie was on the phone with her mother and Mannie. And Martha was tending to her morning duties.

"Okay, and we have everything that we need as far as transportation, direction, and how many books that are going to be distributed with me. The vendor that will be selling, is she in the loop about the time of the event?" I asked all this in one breath.

"Yes, everything is all set to go. You don't have to worry about anything, Corrine." Brenda said.

"Okay, Brenda. Well, I will see you in a couple of weeks. So excited about my first event for the new year. Talk to you later, bye." I said ending the call.

"I love that publicist of yours, girl. She takes care of business." Angie said excitedly.

"Yep, I don't know what I would do without Brenda. She is an inspiration."

"I hear, ya." Angie said drinking the rest of the glass of champagne.

"K.J. would be home tonight. He did not say when, but that he would surprise me." I said to Angie who smiled.

"So, how are you enjoying rekindling the old flame with David Baine?" I asked Angie.

"Somehow, I knew you was gonna go there."

"Yes, you know I really regret the way I treated him in high school. It's as if I needed a reality check and wake up call, he is absolutely keeping my nose open." I said smiling.

"And I can tell from the glow you have, Angie, you are really digging him. I'm happy for you, girl." I said giving her a hug.

"Thanks!" She said.

Looking at my phone my face lit up, I got a text message that the Louboutin store was having a 50% off sell on everything.

"Well let's go!" Angie said.

I grabbed my purse, yelled to Martha that we would be back. Angie raced out the door to my car before I could. Grabbing my keys, I nearly knocked Martha down as she came flying down the steps towards me.

"Where are you off too?" She asked.

"The mall the Louboutin store is having a fifty percent sale on everything and I got somethings I need... Well I don't need, it's me and Angie's favorite store." I said.

"Mrs. Lexington, please be careful." Martha said looking at me.

"And I always do." I said smiling at her grabbing my purse and keys.

"Mrs. Lexington, there's something that I need to tell you."

"Martha, can it wait. I don't want to miss this sale. Everybody and their mother will be at this sale." I said looking at her, trying to get out the door. Martha had this look on her face that was now starting to worry me. "Martha, I'm sure over dinner we can discuss it, whatever it is. I will take it up with you after I come back from the sale." I said.

"Mrs. Lexington, promise me that you will be safe, okay." Martha said as I walked out the door.

"I promise, Martha." I'll be back I said closing and locking the front door.

ANGIE

I was so glad that I had a flight for early Sunday morning. Things were mixed up with Corrine thinking that I was leaving Saturday night. No such thing. She had convinced Martha to stay and cook dinner for us in anticipation of K.J. He had an early arriving plane of 7:00 pm tonight, figuring we could sit, eat, and enjoy my last day with them both before going back home to reality in the early morning. I called David to see how his day had been, we had not spoken since last night.

"Hey, I was just thinking about you." He said answering the phone.

"Well, I'm right on time, I guess." I replied.

"So, you ready to come home?"

"Yeah and no. I have enjoyed my time and I know that Corrine and K.J. will be here in two months for the class reunion. But it was just like old times these past few days I've been here with her."

"Yeah, you two have been friends for years. That's definite friendship right there." David said.

"I know I couldn't have asked for a better sister-friend." I said.

"Can't wait to see you." David said.

"Me either." I replied with a smile.

"Well, I'm on my way to the gym. I'll call you back when I finish." He said.

"Talk to you later."

"Later." He said and hung up. I smiled getting ready to eat a good dinner. Martha was about to prepare a nothing like a home cooked meal. Fast food could be over the top sometimes.

CLASS REUNION

K.J.

I was glad that I was able to make it back home early from L.A. I wanted to at least talk with Angie, she was just like family. Plus, I heard she had rekindled an old flame with David Blaine from high school. He was a real cool dude, him and his people owned two popular soul food restaurants in Chicago. Corrine was so surprised when I told her that I was on an early flight home. I heard Martha was cooking one of her famous home cooked meals. I did not want to miss any of this. I texted Corrine and told her that I would see her in a couple of hours. She texted back and told me "cool".

I purchased the airplane Wi-Fi sitting in coach, I felt a little tired, so I turned on Boney James. Call me an old soul, but when I needed to go to sleep the smooth sound of jazz was the answer to that problem. I dreamt of what the next ten years would hold. Wondering if me and Corrine would have more children. So many possibilities for our lives and I wondered about them all.

CORRINE

It was almost 8:00 pm, Martha was letting the food cool and Angie had just laid Kylie down for me in her room. Martha had made baked macaroni and cheese, potato salad, baked and fried chicken, rolls, and greens. The smell of that food I wanted to ask Martha for a small plate until K.J. got here, but I know she would have said no. Martha was the old school mother type, you would eat when everyone else was there.

I opened my patio door, it was dark and quiet overlooking the Miami downtown. The sky was lit up, it was very beautiful. I was grateful to have Angie here for a few more hours until she went home, and K.J. coming home early it was like old times back when we went to Thornhill. I saw a text message from K.J. letting me know that he was getting off the plane. I texted him back and said see you soon. I smiled as I was looking down at my phone.

Suddenly when I looked up and my expression changed immediately. As I looked into the backyard, I immediately noticed a man in my backyard. As I looked at him closely, I recognized him right away. He was the man that was staring at me during the Orlando book signing event. I could feel the hairs on my neck stand up. Trying to move was not an option because as I stared into the face of the man more memories that I tried to tuck away started flashing before me like a camera. The pain of nearly being raped and beaten, the look on his face when we saw each other for the last time in the courtroom. This was no dream, this was real. He was in front of me staring directly at me. All that I could do right now was shake in fear. I picked up the phone and pushed 911 into the key pad on my phone. That's when Marcus proceeded to walk towards the doors of the house and I ran back inside.

JEFFERY ROSHELL

ANGIE

I was helping Martha plate the food because Corrine had let us know that K.J. was on his way. Suddenly I heard the glass on the front door window shatter. Martha screamed and so did Corrine. I opened the door to find out what was going on and some tall, Black dude dressed in black stood in the middle of the walkway. He was dressed reminiscent of the grim reaper in the Bone Thugz and Harmony Video *Crossroads*. Black long coat, sunglasses, and he had a pistol in his left hand. I ran out of the bathroom into the other room and he left off a shot toward my way. We all screamed. Corrine saw Martha on the other side of the kitchen as she looked down from upstairs.

As I began to assess things something told me that neither, Martha and nor I was the intended target. I watched him walk up the stairs and Corrine ran into her master bedroom closing the door. Martha ran out first, she started yelling at the guy and so did I. He pointed the gun at the both of us. He faked like he was going to shoot us, but then ran up the steps and kicked Corrine's bedroom door in. I heard her scream again.

K.J.

I called Doug and told him to immediately get to my house, something was not right. Corrine never texted me 911 with exclamation points in it. I called another backup driver, named Ron, who would substitute if Doug was not available from time-to-time. It took him less than five minutes to get me out of the airport terminal and on the e-way. I called The Ft. Lauderdale Police and alerted them that something was not right at my home. I explained my wife texted me distress code to inform me something was not okay. They were also in route and on their way. I tried calling and texting, calling and texting, but nothing was going through.

"Tryin' to get there as fast as I can, Kay!" Ron said.

I heard him, but I kept calling and texting, calling and texting, wondering what the hell was going on. "Damn!" I yelled about to throw the phone out the window but wised up.

"Have you talked to Corrine since?"

"Man, no! She was texting me when I got off the plane, then all of a sudden a text came through saying 911! I can't imagine what could be going on." I said in panic mode. My phone rang, and it was Doug.

"Yeah, K.J., I just got to the house. Man, your front door glass is shattered." He said as I heard him running in the house then I heard female voices screaming.

"DOUG! DOUG! MAN, WHAT THE FUCK IS GOIN' ON THERE???" I yelled into the phone.

"K.J., MAN, GET HERE QUICK!" He yelled back but the line went dead. I kept trying to call but it was just ringing.

"Don't worry, bro, we're five minutes away." I heard Ron say.

"BRO, PUNCH IT!" I yelled as he picked up speed.

CORRINE

"Bring your ass out of the bathroom and let me do this the easy way." The hitman said outside the bathroom door in my room. My nerves were all over the place. The only thing I could think of was the fact that my baby, Angie, and Martha were still here in the house, too. I hope K.J. had gotten my message and was on his way.

"BOOM! BOOM!" The knocks on the door came through thunderously.

"I'm going to shoot this muthafukah open if you don't come out." He said just as calm.

"BOOM! BOOM! BOOM!" The knocks came again and this time I screamed.

Then I heard a female voice speak and that's when I heard two gun shots go off and a scream again. I covered my mouth and cried, I didn't know if that was Angie or Martha. But then I heard another male voice and more shots rang out. Then there was a thirty second pause before I heard another voice.

"Corrine! It's Doug, the driver. You can come out." I heard Doug's voice as I opened the door and slowly came out.

"Corrine, you okay?"

"Yes." I managed to say.

"OMG!!!!" I heard Angie scream out.

"Corrine, you might not want to walk around the corner." Doug said giving me a look of warning about what I was going to see.

"CORRINE! ANGIE! DOUG! MAN, WHAT THE FUCK IS THIS????" I heard K.J. yell out.

I rush around Doug to see the man in black lying on his back bleeding from two gunshots to the chest. He laid there with his eyes widow open staring soullessly at the ceiling.

"CORRINE, BABY! STAY THERE." K.J. yelled.

K.J. wasn't able to warn me quickly enough. As I came around the corner I saw Martha lying near the door with a gunshot wound to the chest and head. I let out the loudest wail and dropped to my knees on the floor. Angie and K.J. both came in and hugged me as I cried uncontrollably.

After some time the police finally arrive to the house and discovered the scene. We were all in a terrible shock at the events that went down.

"Mr. Lexington, I know that your wife cannot talk right now, but we need for her to come to the station as soon as possible." I heard the detective say to K.J.

"Understandable, but she's going to need a minute. Our housekeeper is dead. She was like a mother to the both of us. Then we don't know why a hitman was sent here to our house after my wife. This is too unreal."

"WHERE'S KYLIE?" I yelled out.

"I got her, Corrine." Angie said holding and soothing her. I regained my sense of calmness once I was aware that she was safe. As I sat wrap in a sheet numb with no words to say at all.

"Mr. Lexington, do you know if your wife has any crazy fans that could have been up to doing this? The man that entered your home tonight was O'keet Hablama. He is a known hit man from Haiti living here in Miami. Could it be that he was after your housekeeper?" The detective asked.

"I don't know. I mean our housekeeper had been acting quite strange the last few days she was really nervous about something, maybe somebody was after her?"

"Marcus…" I whispered.

"What did you say, baby?" K.J. asked me coming over to the bed to stand near me. Angie was also close by.

"Marcus. Marcus did this." I said still in a daze.

"Who is Marcus?" The detective asked.

"Baby, Marcus is behind bars serving time. What are you talking about?" K.J. asked.

"I saw him tonight. He was in our backyard."

"Corrine, baby, you're scaring me. What are you talking about?"

"Hey Pete, check this out." Another Officer said to the detective that pulled the live video surveillance feed from our monitor on the house.

"Mr. Lexington, let me show you something." Pete the detective said motioning K.J. over to the recorder as the video played.

"That's him!" I heard K.J. say.

"He has changed a lot but that is him." I heard Angie say as well.

"How the hell did he get in my house?" K.J. said.

"Mr. Lexington, we need to gather all the information this guy Marcus. How does your wife know him?"

"She dated him ten years ago. Then sent him to prison for rape and battery charges." K.J. said.

"I will say this, there may be a possible connection to your maid and him as well. We have to find that out so we can find him!"

"So what happens with Corrine?" I heard Angie ask the officers.

"Mrs. Lexington, will have to go into protective custody for a while. We don't know how dangerous this Marcus is, and what he may be capable of doing next. Your wife has to be kept in protective custody until we can locate him or we feel that she is no longer in danger. He sent a hitman to do this job, who knows what's next."

"Corrine, baby, did you hear the officer?" K.J.asked me.

"K.J., I thought this was over. I thought when they sent him away this would never happen again. Now look, Martha is dead! Martha!" I sobbed and held K.J. tight.

"Miss, can you come with us and give your side on what happened as well?" The officers asked Angie.

"Yes, I can. I'm still just as shook up, but I can relay everything I've seen." Angie said sniffling and dabbing at her eyes with the tissue, as she looked over at the coroner taking pictures of the hitman and Martha. Angie walked over to me and rubbed my back. I looked at her then looked back at Martha's body. I was just as puzzled and did not understand why this had happened and to Martha. I tried to block out the images and hearing the gunshots but I couldn't.

"Mr. Lexington, we will have security beefed up here over night."

"I'M NOT STAYIN' IN THIS HOUSE!" I said very loudly.

"Baby, we can go and stay in a room until they put you in protective custody." K.J. said holding Kylie.

"Definitely, we will have security at the hotel of choice as well for the night." Detective Pete said.

"Just give us a minute to get some things together." K.J. said.

"That's fine. By the time we are done with our questions for Ms. Marris I'm sure we'll all be ready to go. We will be back to move you all to a hotel."

"Okay." K.J. said.

"I also need to find out how long Marcus has been out. How he managed to be released so early, and how he was able to find and locate where you all were in Miami. I know that being a ball player, and your wife being well known as well that can play a role."

"I just hope y'all find dude, and get him before I do." K.J. said

"Mr. Lexington, we will work hard to find him - trust me on this." The detective said strongly.

"Okay!" K.J. said to Detective Pete as he and Angie walked out the door to go down to the police station.

Angie had to reschedule her flight because of what happened. She would be leaving some time tomorrow. Doug and Rob both were staying around with loaded pistols, right along with three other Miami officers who were still surrounding the house. The news media had been alerted about the incident, as well as all the local news stations and CNN. There was news reporters planted outside our home. Our families were devastated, especially our mothers at the death of their friend, Martha. It was hard for everyone to understand how such a thing could happen.

"I'm gonna start packing some stuff." K.J. said as he got a bag out.

I got up and started putting a few things in bags as well. It helped in taking my mind off things but I knew that I would not sleep well tonight. While we were still packing some of the authorities that were still on the scene begin to ask us more into Martha's family and possible relatives that lived in the area. I told them that I remember saying some relatives were here from out of town, but didn't know anything else.

My mind was all over the place. My heart was troubled. How did Marcus find me after all these years? Why was I not notified that he was released earlier than what he was supposed to be? I was so worried about where they were going to take me for protective custody. My mind kept picturing scenes from movies about being in some dingy warehouse space and outside of the comforts of the city.

We eventually were all packed and set to leave. We climbed into the black trucks with tinted windows to drive to the secured location. The press was hounding our car attempting to get statements from us. It was a horrific situation. They were snapping pictures of my crying Kylie, and K.J. and I as we tried to hide our faces.

Both our publicist gave statements on our behalf stating that we were safe and cooperating with the authorities to bring justice for the crime. Angie also stepped in and gave a press conference interview for CNN stating that everyone is well also and that when we were ready to speak to the public we would. Eventually, Angie was on her way back to Chicago. We put her on a first class flight and made sure there was enough security with her so that she would not be bothered by all the press commotion.

The next few days were a living hell for me. It finally came time for us to speak to the press about the altercation. It was hurtful to have to relieve the terrifying moments. It reminded me of when

Marcus first attacked me. I did an interview with ABC Nightly News, during the interview I became so enraged that I looked right into the camera and gave a special message to Marcus.

In my nicely designed Chanel suit with my husband and child right beside me, I looked into the camera and said, "They will find you, and put you away, again. This time for good!"

JULY 2010

ANGIE

"Baby, you think Corrine would like this for her birthday gift?" I asked David.

"What is it?" He asked. I showed him the candles I'd purchased from the Candle Barn.

"I guess, that's y'all thing." He said looking at me from my kitchen table shrugging his shoulders.

"Our thing?" I said looking at him.

"Yeah. Hell I don't know nothin' bout candles and smell good that much. Now ask me something about tools and fixing things, and running a restaurant, and I'll give you a good opinion." David said.

"Yeah, yeah!" I said walking to the wall to grab my cordless house phone as it was ringing.

"Angie, what you doin?" My mother asked.

"David is over. We're just looking at some of the things I brought Corrine for her birthday."

"That's right! How are things with her? How has she been?" My mother asked.

"She's been good. She comes out of protective custody next week."

"I know she is happy! She been in there how long?"

"Two and a half months."

"I can only imagine how she feels." My mother said.

"Well, I just want her to enjoy her birthday. Also get ready for our class reunion. You know we only have three weeks to it." I said.

"That's right! It's finally here. Are you excited?" My mother said.

"Yea, I mean, I'm ready to see everybody. But I'm still worried about Corrine. What if he tries to do something to her at the reunion?" I questioned.

"Angie, they gonna catch him. Don't y'all worry. He will turn up soon. Hell, after all this time he may be over it and has moved on from Corrine." My mother tried to console and be optimistic. "I just can't believe he killed Martha. Martha was so nice." My mother said which made me reminisce on that night. As I thought on it tears began to fall out of my eyes.

"I still can't believe it either, ma. The police still believe that Martha was a target. He went after Corrine then when Martha went up into the room they exchanged words. I could not make out what they were saying. The next thing I knew I heard the gunshots and her screams. But I keep wondering why he didn't come after me? Nor did he go after Doug. Something is definitely odd about this situation."

"I'm just glad that you're safe. I also glad that Corrine is too. It could have been worse." My mother said.

"Mama, I know. But this is really crazy and scary. He's still out there, and there's no telling when he might decide to try again." I said as a chill went down my spine. "I recall Corrine describing him. I didn't get a chance to see him, but heard he had the scariest, coldest look ever." I shivered once I thought about it some more. "Mama let me call you back. I have a call coming through." I said hearing the line beep.

Mama said ok, and I clicked the other line.

"Hello." I said.

"Angie?" I heard Corrine say.

"Hey, I was just telling my mama about you. How have you been the last few days?" I asked her in one breath.

"Been okay. But still nervous a bit that the FBI, police, or other detectives on the case can't find Marcus' whereabouts." She said sounding nervous over the phone.

"Corrine, don't worry. I know they will find him. But I understand all of this has to be very hard on you. But they will catch him." I said attempting to reassure her. But I must admit I wasn't fully sure. However, I knew that this was going to take time, but I was here for her.

"Thanks, girl." She said.

"Girl, you know we more like blood sisters then best friends. When you hurt, I hurt."

"I know." Corrine was quiet for a while. I could hear her breathing in the phone and then she spoke again. "To take my mind off things K.J. and I are going to Jamaica for a few days after the reunion. More like a late birthday trip for me. I gotta get back to writing. It just feels like I was isolated from the world longer than I needed to be."

"Well, it's a great thing that you're no longer in isolation." I said laughing.

"Thank, God!" She replied back.

"Well your birthday is going to be a blast. I picked up a few things and I know you're going to love them."

"What you get me?" She asked.

"You'll see." I replied.

"I'm on my way to the New Lenox house. They had me at a discreet location down in the Keys. Girl, I had police outside the bathroom door when I would take a shower. I felt like I was the criminal. There was always someone with me. But thank, God, I could still communicate through phone with everybody, but it really felt like I was in jail."

"Locked up and wouldn't let you out, huh?" I said laughing.

"Yes!" She responded back laughing which I knew eased her worry and made her calmer.

"Well everything with cheering and school is over for a while now that summer is here. I was so sad to see my senior girls go. But I was happy to know they were able to win a championship to end their last year in high school right." I said to Corrine.

"I am so proud that they did it!" She said back.

"Has K.J.'s mom had the baby yet?" I quickly asked.

"No, she is due any minute, though. So at any time she will be giving birth to Rayne Grace." Corrine said.

"That is a pretty name for her, Rayne Grace."

"I helped with it!" Corrine added.

"Baby, tell Corrine I said hello." David chimed in.

"Corrine, David said hi. I almost forgot he was sitting here with me." I said apologizing to him but he understood.

"Hey, David!" Corrine said and I told him.

"Angie, remember when you said that you would never look at David again?"

"Girl, you remember that old shit?" I said acting like I didn't remember it myself.

"Well?" she asked.

"Yes, Corrine, I remember." I said rolling my eyes.

"Look at you now! He's the best thing to happen to you these past months. I say that to say we never know where life is going to take us and with whom. Count your blessings. Just 'cause things did not work out with Gino, they may just work out with David. Trust the process."

"Girl, who are you now? Dr. Damn Phil?" I asked her laughing.

"Whatever, I'm serious, now."

"I hear you. Yes, I am happy and have accepted things now. He still not getting Mannie, they are in Orlando at Disney World. Mannie, Gino, and Gino's new pregnant fiancé."
I said".

"Well, I'm glad that you are moving forward in your love life."

"I just thank God for not counting me out!" I said and Corrine laughed.

"Well, I will call you just as soon as me, K.J., and Kylie land at O'Hare and get to the New Lenox house." Corrine said.

"Okay, girl, call me."

"I will talk and see you soon."

"Be safe!" I said.

"Okay." She replied and hung up the line.

K.J.

I made it to Chicago around 4:30 p.m. with Corrine and Kylie. We were here at the New Lenox house for a few weeks, mainly because our class reunion was coming up soon. The Fahrenheit had a very good season. We made it to our fifth playoff season in a row, but unfortunately we did not bring home the championship this year.

Another big reason we were here in Chicago was because my mom was due any day to give birth to my baby sister. Me and Corrine did not want to miss this for the world. It had been a stressful time from the last few months. Our parents were still on edge about the authorities not able to find Marcus. They just wanted to put the entire ordeal behind us. It was sort of hard to relax knowing a person who tried to kill your wife was on the loose.

I was even more puzzled about why Marcus was able to get paroled. With his violent history he should have never been let out. Also all of his survivors should have been notified. What could he have said to make them believe he wasn't a danger to the public? These were all careless mistakes that the law had made, and at some point I was looking into legal action because of this.

After having to spend two and a half months with my Corrine in protective custody, was very stressful. It affected my life in more ways than one could have imagined. My head was messed up out there on the court. Constantly going in and out of worry about if Marcus might show up at the game, or if my wife was safe while I was in a different city playing. And then to think that my baby girl's life was put in danger. I was ready to kill this man on sight!

As we made it through Terminal E at O'Hare, Carl, our driver and head of security, was waiting to take us to our summer home in New Lenox. Once inside, Corrine held Kylie while she slept and I got on my Blackberry to call my mother.

"Hey, yeah, we made it. Once we get to the house I will give you a call. Okay, love you, bye."

"I know she is ready to push that baby out." Corrine said looking at me.

"Yeah, Rayne ain't ready just yet, but she will be here soon." I said hanging up the phone to check a text message I had coming through.

"Clevon just texted me and asked if him and Shavela could stop by tonight. You feel like company?" I asked her.

"Of course." Corrine said giving me a crazy look.

I texted Clevon back and told him to come by and that we would have food. He texted back and said and mentioned that he would bring a few things as well.

"Let me text Angie to let her know." Corrine said handing Kylie to me.

"K.J., you need anything before I go back in?" Carl asked.

"Naw, Carl, we good, man. Soon as you drop us off you can pretty much call it a night. We got a few friends coming over tonight and more than likely they will probably stay the night." Carl nodded and kept driving.

I listened to Corrine tell Angie about tonight's get-together, and told her to bring David and pack a bag. The drive in wasn't long as Carl turned into the long driveway leading up to our secluded home in New Lenox. This would more than likely be our main house if I ever came back to Chicago and played basketball. We would probably keep the Miami house as a summer home. Once inside, Corrine took Kylie upstairs and changed her. She gave her a bottle and laid her down in her crib. I knew right now was not the time to talk to her about a new nanny, but at some point it would come up. Corrine did not talk much about Martha, and I did not want to bring it up until I was sure she was ready.

I made sure Martha had a proper funeral. I tried contacting family but not one person was able to be located. Even the police tried to gain information about her personal life and they came up with nothing. We did not know where to send Martha's body so we released her ashes on the beach in Ft. Lauderdale.

I took our bags up to our master bedroom and then came back downstairs and sat on the couch with Corrine. I held her in my arms as we sat in silence for a few seconds.

"Baby, it will be okay. They are going to find him." I reassured her.

"Do you think he knows about this house?" Corrine asked.

"I highly doubt it. When you were in protective custody the authorities check the property several times, with surveillance on the house – nothing popped up." I said.

"K.J. I just wish life could rewind. I just wish this was all a dream." I listened to her say.

The funny thing was I really wished for the same, but the reality of it all was that this indeed was not.

THESE LAST PAST TWO AND A HALF MONTHS FELT LIKE YEARS. O'KEETE HAD ONE JOB, AND HE FUCKED IT ALL UP! NOW BECAUSE OF HIS MISTAKE MY MOTHER IS DEAD AND GONE, AND CORRINE WAS STILL ALIVE. IT ANGERED MY SOUL, AND MADE MY HEAD POUND. I CHANGED MY APPEARANCE, MOVED OUT OF THE APARTMENT THAT I HAD IN DADE COUNTY TO ANOTHER LOCATION NOT FAR. I MANAGED TO CHANGE MY IDENTITY.

TWENTY THOUSAND DOLLARS GONE DOWN THE DRAIN. I HAD TO DO TOO MUCH WORK TO GET THE MONEY TO PAY FOR A HITMAN TO DO A JOB HE GOT PAID FOR. I WISH I COULD GET THAT MONEY BACK. BUT

THEY SAY IF YOU WANT SOMETHING DONE RIGHT YOU MUST DO IT YOURSELF.

I OPENED A BOTTLE OF MAD DOG 20/20 AND TOOK A LONG SIP. I ALREADY HAD A PLAN B READY TO TAKE PLACE. IT WAS TIME FOR CORRINE'S CLASS REUNION AND HER BIRTHDAY, BUT I WOULD SAVE THE BIG HIT I HAD FOR THE REUNION.

I ONCE AGAIN HAVE TO PULL OUT MY RESOURCES AND FIND OUT WHERE SHE'S HIDING OUT IN ILLINOIS. IF MOMMA WOULD HAVE ONLY GIVEN ALL THAT I WAS ASKING FOR WHEN SHE WAS ALIVE. I WOULD BE ABLE TO FIND THEM AND TAKE THEM ALL OUT FOR WHAT THEY DID TO MOMMA.

CORRINE

"Happy birthday, dearrrrr, Corrineeee!!!! Happy birthday tooo youuu!!!" The crowd of family and friends sang to me as I blew out the candles and everyone clapped.

"Love you all!" I said crying a little but smiling. July 17th had come very quickly. I was twenty-eight years old.

"Did you wish for a brand new car?" My mother said eyeing K.J. as everyone laughed.

"Yes, mama. I do want a brand new truck, Mr. Lexington." I said looking at him.

"Well, the royalty checks from the publishing house should be coming in. You better cash in on them." K.J. said giving a serious but playful look.

I gave him a face and shook my head. He kissed me on top of my forehead and told me he loved me as everyone aww'd the scene.

"Can we cut this cake?" Angie yelled out.

"Girl, the cake ain't going nowhere." I said to her.

"I know it ain't, but I want a piece." Angie said impatiently.

I shook my head at her and got out a knife and the paper plates to start cutting the cake. It was a red and white butter-creamed icing cake with chocolate on the inside. Shavela had her plate out asking for a nice size piece. I cut it and soon as Clevon saw her with it they started arguing about how she was gaining weight and that piece of cake was gonna add to the pounds on her ass.

"Clevon, don't start with me, and don't show your ass at Corrine's Party!"

"Man, whatever. You're gonna be *Large Marge* after a while, your fat ass keep eating all them sweets and fried fatty foods. I like you thick not morbidly obsessed." Clevon said giving her a very nasty look.

"Fuck you, Clevon!" Shavela yelled.

"Fuck you!!!" Clevon answered back.

"Hey, hey, y'all, cut that out." K.J. said to both Shavela and Clevon.

"Clevon somethin' else!" Angie said looking at him and shaking her head.

"I wish K.J. would talk to me like that." I chimed in.

No matter what the situation was Clevon was wrong for calling her a fat ass. He married her fat ass so he was really out of order for that comment.

"Don't tell his ass nothin', K.J. 'cause the bitch gonna be on the couch tonight!" Shavela yelled out again.

I was glad my party was adult only attendees, but I could tell my mother and father was not fond of the language that was being rattled out.

"I apologize, damn!" Clevon said looking at Shavela.

"Naw, you still better get your ass on that couch." She said.

"Shavela?" I said looking at her.

"My bad, Corrine." She said putting her hands over her mouth.

"Y'all need to hug and make up. All that bickering and arguing, y'all been together too long, and with kids, to be doing that and I bet it's a continuing thing?" My mother said jumping in.

"Mrs. Andersen?"

"Mrs. Andersen, my foot!" My mother said to Shavela giving her a look.

"Now Shavela, Clevon was wrong, baby. I'm not taking his side, but if your husband is asking you to lay off the food and sweets, baby, you need to do that."

"And Clevon?" My mother gave him a stern look.

"Yes, ma'am." He said respectfully.

"Stop cutting your wife down. She is your helpmate, your soul partner. If you didn't love her *fat ass* then you would not have married her. Start treating her like the wife that she is supposed to be treated, not like some woman you know and speak to on the streets. The love needs to be generated more. It's not healthy for you, or your kids." My mother was setting them straight, and they were listening. Both Shavela and Clevon felt some sort guilt over their behavior. "Now y'all both need to apologize to each other and make up." My mother said looking at the both of them. Clevon and Shavela both walked towards each other, exchanged apologies, and hugged. Everyone started clapping as they kissed. "Now see, let that keep going every day and not just at this party. You two been together too long." My mother said.

"Tell them, mama! I'm so tired of it, too." Angie yelled out hugging onto David as everybody laughed.

I smiled thinking and looking at everyone at my party. I was in good company, my guard of being afraid was coming down. Alicia

Meyers' *Say, Say, Say, (You Get The Best Of Me)* came on over the entertainment system and everybody started to dance.

"Can y'all believe in less than two weeks we will be at our ten year class reunion?" Angie said dancing and doing the bump with me.

"Yes!" Both me and Shavela said as we laughed and danced with not a single care about anything.

ANGIE

"Now, how the hell do you want your hair?" My mother asked me as I sat in her shop chair looking through an Ebony Magazine. It was one week before the reunion and right now I was just getting it kinky curled. I was going to put my hair in a high kinky curly ponytail for the reunion.

"Just like that." I said pointing to a picture of Mary J. Blige in the magazine.

"I can do that." My mother said getting ready to curl my hair with the curling iron.

"Is Corrine gonna come in and get her hair done? A few of the girls here been asking about her, wanting to know if she's working on a new book."

"I'll ask her." I said settling back in the seat.

"Angie, I am so happy for you, and I like David. Life really does come full circle. And tell him he needs to start giving me some discounts." She said, as I laughed.

"Yea, we just taking things slow like the John Legend song says." I said.

"Well, I'm sure that slow is gonna turn into something serious. Hell, when we went to dinner I saw the way he looks at you. He has no kids, and never been married? That is a plus, especially with the men we have today."

"Yeah I was pretty shocked that he had not been snatched up. But he almost got there with the last girlfriend he had. But thank God that didn't work out." I said smiling.

"So you know what that means?" My mother asked sounding like she had a smile on her face. I couldn't see because I was in the salon chair with my head away from her.

"No what does it mean, ma?" I asked her.

"That Mannie will not be the only child. You will be giving birth, too. Just don't be like Jeff and Nette, two is enough in my opinion."

"Who said anything about having another?" I said laughing.

"Girl, you know if you marry that man, you're definitely gonna have to give him his own baby."

"I know." I said smiling.

"Long as you do." My mother replied.

I sat back and let my mother work her magic which took her an hour and thirty minutes to do. "Ma, if I did not have you I don't know what I would do." I said looking at myself in the mirror. I looked good.

"You, and especially your brother, would be lost." She said.

317

"I'm just glad you raised me up with the values that you have. Maybe if I'm blessed with a daughter I will definitely do the same thing." I said smiling.

"Maybe. I done told you that you're gonna give that man a baby, and it will be a girl." My mother said smiling.

"And just how do you know that David is the one?" I asked.

"Baby, mama knows. He's gonna be around here for a while. So I hope you're ready for that."

I looked at my mother smiled and said, "I really, really believe that I am."

K.J.

My booking agent contacted me with the information that I
needed for the next week's photo shoot for Nike. I would be away
in L.A. for three days for, and I told him that I definitely had to be
on the plane next Saturday afternoon so I could touch down and go
straight to the class reunion. Baby Rayne still had not made an
appearance, yet. My mother and stepfather did not attend Corrine's
birthday party because my mother was not feeling well. We
thought that was the night Rayne would get ready to make her
appearance but it was a false alarm. I decided to take Corrine out
on a boat cruise in downtown Chicago. It was just me, her, and the
boat as we soaked up the July night heat as she drank a glass of
sangria.

"I will be back in time for the reunion. I told them having me there till Saturday was definitely cutting it close." I explained to Corrine.

"Well, you are the best thing to Nike since Michael Jordan." Corrine said.

"Thank you, baby." I said planting a kiss or her cheek.

"Angie already showed me the dress she worked hard at the gym to get into. David will also be on her arm. She's going to stunt on 'em." I said.

"I already know. Angie ain't changed that much since we was kids." I chimed in drinking my beer.

"Kinda happy I'm home, makes me appreciate how much I miss it here." Corrine said looking out the window over Lake Michigan.

"Yeah, Chicago will always be home." I said.

"Where is the reunion taking place?" I asked her.

"It's going to be at The Gorgio Buccio Banquet Hall."

"That's a good place for it. Nice hall, food should be good, and the area space is nice." I said.

"Well, we shall see. It's finally here next week!" Corrine said.

I know she was just as excited as anyone else ready for the reunion. I ordered another beer and got Corrine another glass of sangria. "Baby, remember how it all started?" I asked her.

"Yep, you were the new boy in P.E. class eighth grade year. I saw you and was immediately in shock as I could not take my eyes off you. Then you gave me your number once class was over and it was history ever since."

"Yep. Never thought I would be married to the girl I dated since eighth grade." I said smiling at her.

Corrine smiled back at me. I felt like the luckiest dude on earth. Not only was my wife beautiful but she was also so accomplished in her own right. We balanced each other out when it came to careers.

"Fate!" Corrine said.

"And the fact that you stuck with my ass." I said laughing.

"Is that so?" She said looking at me.

"Yep. I ain't going nowhere and you're not going nowhere either. You're stuck with me and that's all I have to say about that." I grabbed her hand and went to the middle of the floor as we slow danced to Chaka Khan's *Everlasting Love*.

"Everlasting is what it will be." I said as she laughed. "You can laugh all you want. You know I'm telling the truth." I said hugging her a little tighter listening to Chaka. All that matter was me and Corrine, as we swayed and listened to the music. I realized that this boat outing was much needed.

THERE WERE TWO ARTICLES I PICKED UP FROM MY MOTHER'S HOUSE THE LAST TIME I WAS THERE WHEN SHE WAS ALIVE. ONE WAS HER FIVE THOUSAND DOLLAR NECKLACE THAT I KNEW SHE COULD NOT TAKE TO THE GRAVE WITH HER. WELL SHE WAS PROBABLY TURNING OVER IN HER GRAVE SINCE I TOOK IT AND SOLD IT. AND A BOOK THAT SHE KEPT A BUNCH OF PAPERS IN, THAT UNTIL NOW I HAD NOT HAD THE CHANCE TO GO THROUGH.

SHE HAD ALL TYPE OF PAPERS IN IT. I HAD NO IDEA WHAT I WAS EVEN DOING WITH IT. I HAD TO QUESTION MYSELF WHY THE FUCK WOULD I TAKE THIS BOOK? I

NEEDED TO THROW THE SHIT OUT AS IT HAD NO

SIGNIFICANCE FOR WHAT I NEEDED IT FOR.

LOOKING AND LOOKING, SAME SHIT, BILL AFTER

BILL AFTER BILL. THEN THERE WERE THINGS THAT SHE

HAD JOTTED DOWN. THINGS LIKE WHAT SHE WAS

MAKING FOR DINNER FOR THAT BITCH AND HER

FAMILY ON A GIVEN DAY. THEN THERE WAS OTHER

THINGS LIKE CHURCH AND HOW SHE HAD PLANNED TO

GIVE TO A STRUGGLING FOUNDATION FOR TEENS IN

DADE COUNTY. BORED WITH IT, I SAT IT DOWN, THEN A

PIECE OF PAPER THAT WAS FOLDED CAME OUT THE

SIDE FLAP OF THE BOOK. I GRABBED IT BEFORE IT FELL

TO THE FLOOR. I UNFOLDED IT FROM THE FOUR WAYS

THAT IT WAS FOLDED AND OPENED IT.

I IMMEDIATELY SMILED WHEN I SAW THE GIFT THAT

THE DEVIL PLACED IN FRONT OF ME. I WAS

OVERJOYED AS I SAW THE ADDRESS TO THE HOME

THAT CORRINE AND K.J. OWNED IN NEW LENOX. I

LAUGHED AND LAUGHED, TAKING A LONG SWIG OF

THE HENNESSY BOTTLE AND SLAMMED IT DOWN ON THE TABLE. I PICKED UP THE CORDLESS PHONE ON THE WALL AND DIALED OUT.

"THANK YOU FOR CALLING SOUTHWEST AIRLINES MY NAME IS CASSANDRA AND HOW CAN I HELP YOU TODAY?"

"YES CASSANDRA, MY NAME IS JOHN PROVENT AND I AM LOOKING FOR A FLIGHT TO CHICAGO FROM MIAMI AIRPORT. CAN YOU HELP ME WITH RESERVATIONS PLEASE?"

"SURE, NO PROBLEM, JOHN. WHEN ARE YOU THINKING OF TAKING THE TRIP?"

"HOW ABOUT TOMORROW MORNING IF I CAN?"

"YOU SURE CAN ARE YOU READY TO PROCEED WITH INFORMATION AND FLIGHT BOOKING?"

"YES, LET'S GET STARTED." I SAID AS I GRABBED THE CREDIT CARD THAT WAS IN MY WALLET. I BOOKED MY FLIGHT. I WAS JUST IN TIME FOR THE CLASS

REUNION. IT WAS TIME FOR ME TO DO WHAT I SHOULD

HAVE DONE IN THE FIRST PLACE MYSELF.

CORRINE

"Mama, I am going to bring Kylie by your house before I head to the reunion. Angie is meeting me there. K.J. will coming straight from his flight from LAX." I said to my mother over my cell phone as I brushed my hair and laid out my dress for the night.

"I will be waiting." My mother said enthusiastically.

"You okay with being at that house by yourself?" My mother asked.

"Yes. Security has been here twenty-four-seven and Carl has been here on the premises throughout the day. He's going to be driving me that way, and also picking K.J. up from the airport once he drops me off."

"Okay, well I'll be waiting on you and my Kylie-baby."

"We will be there soon, mama."

"Okay, love you."

"Love you, too, mama. See you soon." I said hanging up the phone.

I had already showered. I sprayed some perfume on, started putting on my makeup, and made sure my hair was intact. Angie's mom had hooked my hair up for the reunion. I smiled in mirror applying my lipstick and earrings. I definitely was going to make a stunning appearance tonight, just like I did for prom.

"Mrs. Lexington, will you be ready soon? It's working on 6:30 pm." Carl said trying to make sure he keeps up with the time.

"Yes, I'm grabbing Kylie, the baby bag, my purse, and phone." I said going into Kylie's room grabbing her. I eventually made my way down the stairs and out to the waiting truck. "Carl, you didn't put the baby seat in the back?" I said as he sat in the front. I looked for him to answer and he didn't. "Carl?" I called to him again.

I closed the door and went around to the front of the truck's driver side. When I got around there my eyes popped out of my head and I let out a loud scream. Kylie startled and went into a loud cry of fear. Carl had a gunshot wound to his chest with eyes wide open. My heart started pounding. With Kylie in my arms I ran as best I could back into the house locking the door. I laid her down on the couch as she was still crying hysterically.

"911. What's your emergency?" The 911 operator said.

"Yes, I need a unit to come to twenty-two…" I screamed and dropped my cellphone as the glass shattered from the kitchen door leading to the outside. I felt myself being grabbed with a bear hug from behind.

ANGIE

I stepped out of David's all black, Eddie Bauer truck in the dress that I spent the last couple of months putting myself through hell at the gym and eating all the right foods to get into. I had a pair of Jimmy Choo matching heels. David had on an expensive pair of dress slacks, Stacey Adams, and had just gotten his hair cut. He finished his outfit with a dressy red button up to go with. I was feeling myself as I sashayed my way to the front door of the Gorgio Buccio Banquet Hall with him alongside me.

"You ready?" He asked me.

"Ready as I will ever be." I said back as we got to the front entrance and he held the door open for me.

"Hello welcome to the reunion!" The hostess said. Once she got a good look at me she recognized me, "Oh my God Angie!!!" She yelled. It was Taylor Garrett who was on the cheerleading team with me back in high school.

"Taylor???" I said as we hugged each other. Taylor looked good, she put on a little weight but it fit her. She cut her hair short which also complimented her. The dress she was wearing was a killer - she was here to show out as well.

"Have you seen Corrine yet?" I asked her.

"No. I thought that she might make an entrance with you?" Taylor asked.

"Naw, I came with David."

"David Baine?" Taylor said shocked giving him a hug.

"Are you guys dating?" Taylor teased.

"Yeah, something to that effect." David said smiling at me and I smiled back.

"Congrats, this is my husband, Tavis." Taylor said introducing us to a tall, thin, light-skinned attractive guy with glasses. We share a little bit of small talk with Taylor and her husband. They showed us picture quickly, and then David and I went into the reunion.

"Looks really nice." David said looking around.

"Damn, I don't really know who is who unless people come up to me." I said looking around. David and I made our way to the buffet where it was traditional fixing of soul food and a cake that read, "Congratulations Thornhill High School Class of 2000 Ten-Year Reunion".

I saw Shavela and Clevon coming up. Shavela smiled which meant she spotted me. She was wearing a nice dress skirt and top that she had managed to lose weight to get into as well. My mother also hooked up her hair with a nice style that made her look youthful, but also gave her a mature look.

"Hey!" Shavela said hugging David and greeting me.

" Hey you talk to Corrine yet?" I asked her hugging Deon.

"Naw, not since earlier." I said.

"K.J. said that his plane should land at O'Hare in an hour." Clevon said.

"Well maybe they decided to come together." I said and everyone agreed.

"Who did the food? Hell, that shit looks good!" Shavela said and Clevon gave her a look and shook his head.

"I did!" David spoke and we all looked at him.

"Courtesy of BeeBee's!" He said with a smile.

"Well damn, let me get a plate!" Shavela said going over to the table.

"Ai'ight, that dress gonna buss." Clevon yelled out and we all laughed.

I grabbed a small plate and put on a few light items to eat. I didn't want nothing too heavy as I wanted to remain comfortable in my dress. I sat and talked with Shavela for another twenty minutes and still no K.J. or Corrine.

"I'ma try calling her." I said dialing out on my phone.

It rung and went straight to voicemail. I left her a message telling her to give me a call as soon as she could. The reunion had started already and we were definitely waiting for her and K.J., they were both our Prom King and Queen.

"Just give it a minute, like Clevon said he spoke to K.J. So he probably headed home to get ready while Corrine is waiting. And you know they have to drop Kylie off at her mama's. So let's just give them some time." Shavela said.

"That's right." I said to myself as Deon and Judy, his girlfriend, walked up to greet us.

Me and Shavela hugged Judy then Deon, and we all started talking amongst ourselves with them asking where K.J. and Corrine was. I felt the presence of a man come up behind me as we all turned around. I looked like I had seen a ghost. Standing in front of me was Daniel. He was a male cheerleader who cheered with us in high school.

"Angie, Shavela?" He calls out our names.

"Daniellllllll!!" Shavela screamed and hugged him.

"Daniel, look at you man." I said coming in to give him a hug right after her.

"Y'all look good, too" He said smiling.

Daniel had adorned dreads, which appeared to be freshly twisted. He had to be a gym nut because he was cut up, muscles everywhere. He wore a fitted shirt and slacks told that story of how fit he was. And the cologne he was wearing was definitely a handsomely, complementary fragrance, which was Dolce & Gabbana Blue – he smelled so dreamy.

"Corrine here yet?" He asked.

"Naw, she will be though." Shavela and I said together.

"I'm going to speak and say hi to everyone else. I'll come back." Daniel said.

"Cool, we should still be here." I said watching him walk off to mingle.

"Damn, he don't even look gay as hell no more." Clevon said laughing.

"Don't start!" Shavela said giving him a look.

"I mean, I ain't talking about him. Shit, if he a fag, he a fag, but he look like he not no more." Clevon said shrugging his shoulders at everyone. Deon just looked, and David did the same.

"Well, gay or not, the boy looks damn good!" Shavela said.

"You can take your ass home wit' him tonight!" Clevon said to her making a face.

"Whatever!" Shavela said back.

The D.J. started spinning Toni Braxton's *He Wasn't Man Enough For Me* and coming through the front entrance as we all turned our heads was Shana and her must have been woman that played for the WNBA, looking like a fake ass Bonnie and Clyde couple.

"That chick looks like a fine ass man." Shavela said shaking her head.

"Damn, Shana still lookin' good, too!" Clevon said and Shavela gave him a dirty ass look.

"Lookin' like the hoe she was in high school. And if you keep battin' them eyes im'a slap them out your head." Shavela said to Clevon as we all laughed out loud.

"Stop trippin', I'm only playin'".

"Whatever, nigga!" Shavela said rolling her eyes.

"Well, Clevon ain't got to worry about that, hell she ain't thinkin' about no man!" I said looking at Shana and the girl walk around holding hands like a newly married couple greeting everybody.

"Where in the hell is Corrine and K.J.?" I said out loud.

"It's working on 7:30, we been here almost an hour and a half." Shavela said.

"Let me call, Kay." Deon said taking out his cell phone and dialing out.

"Aye waddup, bro! Yo, where you at?" Deon pauses, then his face scrunches up. "Aww, shit, really! Damn, that's wassup! Congrats on that! Yeah we all here! Naw, bro, Corrine ain't here, man! Yeah and she not answering either. Ai'ight, ai'ight, peace." Deon said hanging up.

Deon turns to us and gives us the news. "Well K.J.'s mom just gave birth to his little sister so that's where he is coming from now, the hospital. But for some reason he thought that Corrine was already here, and she's not. He said he was about to call her mom's house cause she not answering for him either."

I was happy for K.J.'s mother, but something was not right. Corrine would have texted at least to say she was running late. She should have been here by now. I just truly hope she got caught up at her mother's house.

K.J.

I left the Community Hospital where my mother was. She had given birth to my little sister two hours before I had gotten off the plane. She was so cute, had a head full of hair, and just as chunky as she wanted to be. Kylie now had an aunt younger than her. Wow, I was so happy for my mother and Walter. I called Corrine and still no answer from her. I was getting a little worried because Deon had told me she wasn't at the reunion yet. I was on my way to the reunion, just knowing she would be there waiting on me when I got there.

"Thanks." I said to my personal driver.

"No problem, Mr. Lexington." He said letting me out the back seat of the truck. I walked up the steps of the banquet hall and was greeted all of my former classmates. Some I remembered, others I had to guess who they were. As I made my way through the reunion, I saw Deon, Clevon, Shavela, Angie, David, and Judy all standing around the bar area. I walked up and everyone's attention was on me.

"Bro, we have been waiting. Where's Corrine?" Deon asked.

"I thought she was here already." I said.

"No!" Angie said looking very suspicious at me now.

I didn't know what was going on but I was about to find out. I called Corrine's mother and she said that she was expecting Corrine over and hour ago. I told her that I would call her back quickly. I called Corrine's phone and it rang, this prompted me to leave her a message.

"Baby, it's K.J., where are you? Call me ASAP!" I said hanging up.

I stood for a second, told everyone that I would be back and stepped outside. I don't know what opted for me to call the house phone at the New Lenox house but I did. After two rings the line answered.

"Baby! It's K.J., what are you doing? Why are you not at the reunion????" I got all that out in a three second breath. There was no answer. "Corrine? Hello? Hello?" I said listening to silence, then an eerie laugh came over the line.

"K.J., man, wassup?! Corrine can't talk right now she's tied up!"

The blood in my body boiled and my stomach was in the tightest knot, knowing who that voice belonged. I spoke back immediately, "If you hurt her or my baby, it won't be the police that your ass is gonna have to worry about!"

"Threats don't bother me, nigga!" Marcus shouted back.

"I don't make threats! That ass beatin' I gave you ten years ago in that hallway wasn't enough, huh? You ready for me to bury your mothafuckin' ass!" I spat out over the phone and he laughed.

341

"Tell you what? You got an hour to get your ass to this house, or I kill this bitch and your baby. If I see the cops I'ma shoot them and me. Choice is yours." He said and the line went click. I hung up my phone walked towards the door and out the entrance. I could hear Deon, Clevon, Angie, and Shavela calling my name but I just kept walking. I got in the truck and told the driver to get me to my house as fast as he could.

CORRINE

I blinked and opened my eyes. I could tell I was in my home but did not know what room I was in. I had a serious headache and a bruise on my head and hand. The right side of my body was in so much pain. I coughed and blinked as I heard footsteps and then the light in the room came on quickly. I was upstairs in the attic part of the house. I saw Marcus with a gun in his hand walking toward me. I tried to sit up but noticed that my hands were tied in a small knot. He looked at me, and then knelt down beside me. He took a small pocket knife and cut the tied knot that was around my hands.

"If you move I will stick this knife in that baby's neck!" He said giving me an evil look that made me nervous on the inside.

"WHERE IS MY BABY!?!" I yelled at him looking around the room not seeing or hearing Kylie.

"She's alive." He said looking at me. "I don't have to explain to you why I am doing this. You already know. I spent the last eight years planning this out. Having your head on a stick has been the goal ever since I got sent to prison when you testified against me in court. Now I get my revenge." He said smiling.

"Fuck you!" I screamed at him. He knelt down and back hand slapped me so hard I blanked out and started coughing blood.

"Bitch! Did I tell you to speak! No, I didn't. So shut the fuck up! That's your fuckin' problem now!"

I started to cry a little. I was praying that Kylie was still alive and nothing had happened to her. I didn't hear any sign of her and that was not good. "Please, God, let K.J. get to me." I cried out.

"Your man is supposedly on his way. I told him if I see a cop with him, I'm going to put a bullet in both, you and the baby's head. And I'll kill myself and not give him the satisfaction of revenge. I don't have shit to live for getting caught."

344

"You are one sick muthafuckin' individual." I said to him through clenched teeth.

"And you keep talking, you're gonna be one dead little bitch!" He replied back cocking his gun and pointing it at me.

"Why did you have someone kill our maid?" I said to him as I saw his eyes get really big and a smile crept across his face.

"Funny you ask that. It's definitely time for you to know the truth on things, especially before you die tonight. Martha, your precious loving maid, was my damn mother! She did not know that you were the one that sent me to jail until I told her. It was too late to go to you about it because she knew you would have fired her on the spot. I figured it out when I came to visit her back when she first started working for you. She immediately told me to go on with my life and to never make any contact with you. She valued her job and loved you! That tore me up on the inside because she never, ever, told me that she loved me. Hell, she sent me away when I was a kid! Told me I was no good! I couldn't stand it! So I took matters into my own hands and proceeded to start my plan to kill you. When she found out she started to threaten me with the police. I knew at that point she would stand in the way. She left me no choice but to hire a hitman to carry out the job. As you can see he missed his target, it's fucked up, but for some reason I knew she had it coming to her."

"Martha!" I yelled out bawling my eyes out.

"You act like she was your damn mama." Marcus said shaking his head and laughing. He pointed the gun in my face. "Your man got less than fifteen minutes to get here."

"And killing me is going to accomplish what?" I asked him as I gained control of my feelings and calmed myself enough to speak.

"I will have won. In the end I will have finally won." He said getting down in my face and smiling at me. That's when the alarm system announced that the front door had opened and I heard K.J.'s voice.

"Corrine! Corrine! Where you at baby??? Where is Kylie???" He yelled out.

"If you say anything I will blow your fuckin head off! Shut up!" Marcus said running out of the room. I nervously shook and didn't say anything. Suddenly I hear the door opened and in came K.J.

"Baby! Baby! Are You Okay!!!!???" He asked me trying to hold and hug me seeing the bruises on my face, head, and hand. I held onto him and shook, but screamed when I saw Marcus bring down a bat and knocked K.J. over the head. Tears streamed down my face. I looked up at Marcus with an angered rage; he caught it and returned it with a smile on his.

"Now I have the both of you right where I want you!"

ANGIE

I caught K.J.'s drift and knew that something definitely was not right the way he rushed out of there. Between Shavela, Deon, and Clevon wondering if they should follow him or leave it alone, I took on the liberty to call my brother Jeff on my phone.

"Yeah, ain't you at your class reunion?" He asked.

"Yes, but something ain't right. I need you to get up here and take a ride with me to Corrine and K.J.'s in New Lenox."

"Why? What's going on?"

"Just do what I said and get here quick! Bring your gun, and once we start making our way out there call the police." I said.

"I'll be there in five minutes." Jeff responded back as I ended the call.

"I'm going to take a ride with my brother. I'll be back." I told David.

"Angie, is everything okay?" David said looking at me suspiciously.

"It will be." I said walking out toward the entrance doors to wait for Jeff.

K.J.

I thought maybe it was God I was seeing, then maybe it was just a bright light. I reached out in the brightness but was unable to grab a hold of it. I heard Marcus talking to Corrine as I laid on the floor playing like I was still knocked out. Thinking of something quick, I prayed that he didn't shoot me while I laying down. I needed to be as discreet as possible so that I could snake his ass real good. I heard Corrine's phone ring. Marcus picked up the phone and I could hear Angie calling out for Corrine in the background.

She was telling Corrine that she was on her way out there, but Corrine kept begging her not to come. I cursed myself for not having my gun on me. Foolishly, I sent the driver away because I did not want Marcus thinking he was the police. I continued to lay still and waited to see how this was going to play out. I knew this was going to go in the right favor, but just how? Was the question.

CORRINE

"Angie, please do not come here, just go back!" I yelled at her on my cellphone.

"Corrine I am walking up the steps of your door about to come in now. Is Marcus in there?" She asked me. Marcus looked at me and went to hide.

I knew this was not going to go well. For one, he took his loaded gun this time instead of the bat. And for two who knows where he was hiding and if he was going to shoot Angie with it.

"Corrine, what room are you in? This house is fuckin' dark as shit!" I heard her say.

"Angie, just go, just go!" I yelled looking over at K.J. who did not budge one second. I did not know whether he was unconscious or dead.

"Corrine, I think I know where you are." I heard her say coming up the steps.

"Angie! Go! Marcus is here!"

"Corrine, I don't give a fuck about Marcus!" She yelled back. I heard her by the door and she came right on in.

"Corrine! Oh my, God! Look at you! Damn look at K.J.! Shit! Where is Kylie???" Angie said in one breath with her eyes bugged out of her head.

"You need to get out of here!" I said to her.

"I don't need to do shit!" She said back.

"Angie, please. He's gonna kill you, too."

"Corrine, I gotta get you out of here and we gotta find Kylie." She said coming over to me.

I started to say something to her when Marcus rushed into the room and jumped on her. I screamed and jumped up, jumping on his back. He started whirling me around like a person riding the mechanical bull at the bar. He threw me off, grabbed his gun and started shooting, but missed Angie.

Suddenly K.J. jumped up and Marcus turned around and shot him twice in the chest area and he went crashing back out the window. I screamed, Marcus looked at me but went after Angie who had ran out of the room soon as he started shooting at her.

"Where that bitch of a friend of yours go? O'keete should have offed her ass that night, too!" Marcus said running out the room with the gun in his hand.

I stood up looked at the broken window that K.J. went through, slowly walking over to it to look out of it. My hand over my mouth, I cried and blinked twice. I blinked again, looking out the window and down to the ground. K.J. was not there. I took another double take, but I was sure he was not there. I looked towards the door and found the strength to run out of it myself.

JEFFERY ROSHELL

ANGIE

Seeing that I'd been to Corrine's house so many times, I knew every crawl space and hiding place there could have been. Call me a cat with nine lives because I don't really know how I just dodged three bullets, especially in the dress I was in. But thank you, Jesus for the gym and the fact that Jeff brought me a pair of Nette's New Balances to put on. I texted Jeff and told him that Marcus was on the move. He texted back and told me that he had caught up to K.J. and the police were in route.

Now all I had to do was find out where Marcus' ass was. I slowly crept out of my hiding place careful not to make a sound. Suddenly I saw him come out of the room in front of me walking. I quickly stopped in my tracks, but he did the same. I had to think swiftly. My goal was to knock the gun out of his hand. I guess I had been watching too much CSI because that's where the thought came from. I saw a lady do it before on the show to distract her killer.

I could tell he was listening to hear where I had gone. That's when I picked up speed, yelled out and kicked the gun out of his hand. He turned around swung at me but missed. I kicked him dead on in his dick and balls. Grabbing them he called me a bitch and tried to lunge at me. I tried to kick him again but lost my balance and fell. That's when he jumped on me and started chocking me. I could not grab anything to hit him with and I began coughing.

After a while, I heard Corrine scream and she came running in. He lost track of thought with me and I moved back enough from him to kick him in the nose, blood squirted everywhere as he screamed out. He grabbed me by my arm and flung me over Corrine's banister, the last thing I heard was her scream as I went down and hit the ground.

K.J.

I wore a bullet proof vest that I snuck off my driver/body guard. Marcus underestimated that I would come prepared. There were other vests in the truck so I was able to take one and give it to Jeff who was hiding in the house. When I came crashing out the window I hit the ground hard but it wasn't enough to knock me cold out. Marcus thought he had got me, but he was one stupid muthafuckah, he should have gone for the head.

"We need to kill this muthafuckah before he kills one of us." I said to Angie's brother in a whisper.

"Yea, man." Jeff said holding his gun. We saw Marcus taking Corrine outside by the arms toward the other side back of the house, but where was Angie?

"Man, where's my sister?" Jeff said running into the house making sure not to bring attention to himself. I ran behind him and we both stopped dead in our tracks as we saw her lying in the middle of the floor with her eyes shut.

CORRINE

"I'm going to shoot you execution style, bitch! Then plant the gun on your dead husband. He went a little mad and killed you and your girlfriend is the plan." Marcus said laughing.

"You will not get away with this." I said.

"Wanna bet? Say hello to my mother for me." He said backing up from me and then cocking the gun, pointing it at my head.

I closed my eyes waiting on the worse then I heard a voice from behind him tell him to "drop the muthafuckin' gun or they was going to put him face down in the ground"! I immediately recognized the voice, it belong to Jeff.

"I thought I told that muthafuckah no cops!!!" Marcus yelled out.

I quickly ran away before he thought to shoot me. Jeff shot Marcus three times taking him down. He fell down beside the tree, and I ran over to Jeff.

"Corrine, are you okay?" He asked me examining me to make sure I was ok.

"Yes!" I cried in a relief that it was finally over.

"Corrine!" K.J. yelled running out of the house. "I found Kylie! She was in the hamper where the clothes were! She's okay!" He said kissing her forehead.

I tried to walk toward him to get her. In a flash Jeff yells out, "Corrine look out!"

In one last attempt to get to me Marcus lifts up, but Jeff quickly gets a shot off into the forehead and chest of Marcus. Suddenly we hear the sound of a car coming rapidly from the front toward the back area where we were.

"MUTHAFUCKAHHHHHHHHHH!!!" We hear Angie

scream as she ran Marcus into the tree with the front of Jeff's car.

Blood gushed out of his mouth, parts of his stomach and chest

were on the car and he lay on the hood. We heard the police sirens

and the cops came rushing around to the back, as we all stood and

looked on at the dead body lying across the hood of the car.

TWO MONTHS LATER..............

"So, Corrine, you are now speaking about your ordeal of how the man you sent to prison when you were a teenager, got out on a lesser sentence, tried to kill you, but ended up dead himself. Then to find out his very mother was your live-in maid! That's a storyline for a book, don't you think?" I heard Tonya Winters, the CNN News Anchor say on her 6:00 pm show.

"Yes, Tonya. This has all been a very drastic, but quick mending change for me, my husband, and my best friend. We all lived this ordeal that night in July. But we managed to get ourselves back to where we were and things are on the up-and-up!" I said smiling at her.

"And how is your best friend, Angela?"

"She's doing great. She came out with sprained wrist in the nightmare but she's back on track. She teaching at our old school, and even rekindled a new love with a high school classmate of ours, I am proud of her."

"And K.J.?" Tonya asks.

"K.J. is K.J. He's just like me, glad this is all over with. We made sure that Marcus was dead as they picked up his body and took him away. They even said cremating him would be a choice as well. He has no known immediate family, and I can now finally close that chapter of my life and move forward for good." I said to Tonya.

"And I am certainly happy for you. Happy that you came out of that alive and well. Like I said, I'm looking for the tell-all book, honey. 'Cause, chile, that's a story in itself!" Tonya said and we both laughed.

"Well, I am glad to have talked to you. Corrine, I wish you nothing but continued success in life, waiting on the book, and is there anything you want to say before leaving this segment with me?"

"Yes, I got ten years 'til my next *class reunion* and I won't be missing that for the world!"

Acknowledgements

So here it is, 8:09 pm on Saturday, October 6, 2018, and this book should have been edited and published months ago. Part of the publishing delay was my procrastination. I always pride myself on being timely and doing things in a fashionable manner – but this particular story took more out of me than usual. So sincerely, my apologies to the readers who have been anticipating the release of this book for months!

I cannot believe I've been writing for four years. I take none of this experience for granted. These Thornhill Kids have taken me on quite a journey, but I'm sorry to tell you this is it for these kids! They're all grown up! They have kids and need to focus on their families and personal lives!

If we could fast forward from 2010 to 2018 a lot of things about our group would have changed. Corrine and K.J. would have a son, in addition to Kylie. Angie and David would be well off and married with a child of their own. And Mannie would be seventeen entering into his junior year of high school and still living with his mother. He wouldn't dare leave Angie alone to live with his daddy with no supervision. Gino would be divorced from the woman he married and they would have had two additional children during their marriage. Shavela and Clevon would still be together, and so would Jeff and Nette. I could go on and on, but this is how things would play out! So there you all have it! Your happily-ever-after ending for those Thornhill Kids.

Well, let me get to thanking a few folks…

As always I have to thank God for giving me the grace of writing. Without his guidance, understanding, and wisdom I am nothing in front of my laptop! My Aunt Youvonn High for her Proofreading skills, with the first read, Love yah!

My author brothers and sisters! It is so many of you all, old and new that there's not enough paper to name everyone. So I'll keep it simple and say personal thank you's to those I have the most constant and true genuine friendship with.

Author Ty Waller, my editor, sister, and rock. This is someone in the writing world I can lean on when things get hard. Thank you for putting up with me and pushing me to go higher each with each new novel that I write.

Candace Andersen, Leeandra Frazier, and Paul Nickerson thank you guys for making Corrine, Angie, and K.J. come to life on the revised cover of *Thornhill High School* and *Class Reunion*. I am forever grateful to you three for that! Jeff, whom I affectionately call (Jhitz), my best homeboy, thank you for both revised covers. I'm grateful for April Freeman because of her, we have been close since day one! The connection was divine.

Shanelle Harris for the constant push of wanting to know what happened since I left her hanging at the end of *Thornhill High School*. I hope you enjoy *Class Reunion* and things turn out how you projected.

I thank Vicki and Marilyn Bell.

Kenya Ervin for that powerful and beautifully written foreword.

Soul Sistah's Book Club, Janice Elmore and The South Holland Public Library. Toneal Jackson and APS Books, and Theresa Browning (aka Mz. Author T).

Rowash Publishing, I couldn't do it without you!!! My mother, Elfreda Jones, stepfather, Alfred Jones, my youngest sister, Jennifer Roshell, and my Washington and Roshell Family. The Elersons, Marshalls, Clays, Sykes, and anyone close to those families - I love, appreciate, and thank you!

My Pastor and First Lady Edwin & Beverly Harris, Radiah Hubbert, and Ashantay Keys.

My immediate author brothers and sisters, Sakeena Raheem, Shadawne Barner, Andre Johnson, Shawn Starling, Joe Awesome, Caryn Lee, Shoney K, Quintessa Turner, Jaz Akins, Author Le'vonne, Jessica Watkins, Ebony Abby, Sherrod Tunstall, Danielle Vann, Shanee Norfleet-Brown, and Verlean Singletary.

And especially to you, who took the time to read this novel. I hope you enjoyed just like the others, stay tuned for the next one. 'Till then, peace, love, and blessings!

I've given myself a two-to-three week break before I start my next novel, *All Marvin's Children*. I believe this will be another award-winner just like *It's Gonna Rain*!

Also be on the lookout, *Friday After Dark II* will drop in 2019 as well......

JEFFERY ROSHELL

ABOUT THE AUTHOR

Jeffery Roshell is the author of novels, *Thornhill High School*, *It's Gonna Rain*, and *Friday After Dark*.

He lives in Chicago, Illinois where he is at work on his next novel. You can reach out to him on Facebook@ his Author Jeffery Roshell page and Instagram @authorjefferyroshell

Made in United States
North Haven, CT
30 June 2023

38412751R00212